THE
BURNING
LIGHT

By Betsy Ramsay

The Burning Light

Published by Pitspopany Press
Text Copyright © 2002 by Betsy Ramsay
Illustrations Copyright © 2002 by Avi Katz

Cover Design by Benjie Herskowitz
Book Design by Tiffen Studios (T.C. Peterseil)

Hard Cover   ISBN: 1-930143-43-5
Soft Cover   ISBN: 1-930143-44-3

Pitspopany Press titles may be purchased for fund raising programs by schools and organizations by contacting:

Marketing Director, Pitspopany Press
40 East 78th Street, Suite 16D
New York, New York 10021
Tel: (800) 232-2931
Fax: (212) 472-6253
Email: pitspop@netvision.net.il
Web Site: www.pitspopany.com

Printed in Israel

TABLE OF CONTENTS

TABLE OF CONTENTS

To my three children,
Gail, May and Anders

And my three grandchildren,
Anna, Astrid, and Alice

It was unmistakable –
a little jar all caked with dirt.

THE
BURNING
LIGHT

WE COULD BE HEROES!

The rain had stopped and a hazy pink glow filled the Tel Aviv sky. Inside the narrow living room of the fourth-floor apartment, Hanukkah lights were glimmering, their shadows dancing playfully on the wall.

As Galit, Gidon and little Amos watched the flickering candles, the two older children talked about the first Hanukkah that was ever celebrated, when the Temple was rededicated over two thousand years before. They had seen a movie about it in school the day before and the exciting images were still fresh in their minds.

"I wish I'd lived in those days," Gidon sighed dreamily, slumping into the flowery cushions in the faded wicker chair.

Gidon, almost nine, was a thoughtful boy. He liked adventure stories. He often imagined the great things he would do one day. His sister, Galit, two and a half years older, was more down-to-earth and practical. She wasn't sure Gidon would ever accomplish the great things he talked of. He spent so much time doing nothing but dreaming when he might as well have been playing basketball or soccer with his friends. Even so, he was the fastest runner in the school.

"You wish you'd lived *when*, Gidon?" Galit responded, astonished. "This is one of your daydreams. You don't know what you're talking about when you say things like that."

Galit was a girl with a lot of spunk and toughness.

She, too, was always ready for an adventure or a healthy challenge. But the adventure had to "make sense." This one didn't.

"Who would want to live in those days?" she asked, skeptically. "Jewish people were being killed like flies. Children were tortured. You saw it in the movie!"

"Who would want to? I would!" her brother insisted. "Judah Maccabee was a hero. We could have been heroes, too. I'd like to be a hero for a great cause."

"There aren't any heroes nowadays, dummy. You've gotta' be kidding. Do you want to die for being Jewish like Aunt Bertha at Auschwitz?"

"No. Of course not."

"Gidon, living in the days of the Maccabees is a crazy idea."

"It isn't either. I wouldn't even mind *dying*, if it's for something good."

"There's no such thing as dying for something good," Galit told him.

"Yes, there is! Think of Yoni Netanyahu. He died at Entebbe saving all those hostages. Besides, we might not have to die. Remember in the movie? The Maccabees fought when things seemed hopeless and outsmarted their enemies. God helped them!"

"It's true. They believed in God and He didn't let them down. But don't forget how hard it was, Gidon. Lots of our people didn't want to suffer for being Jewish. They followed the Greek customs just to be safer and to please the Greeks."

"They were traitors!"

"They were."

"I'd rather die than be a traitor! The Maccabees

knew that they might get killed any day, but they followed the Jewish taechings."

Galit didn't answer. She was thinking of something else. When lighting the first Hanukkah candle that evening, her father had talked of the courage and faith shown by Mattityahu Maccabee and his sons.

"That's why the Jews are free today," he had said. "If they hadn't been brave for God, there might not be any more Jews."

A warm feeling flooded Galit's heart as she thought about it. She also remembered what her Father had said about the *Shamash*, the middle candle.

"Gidon, remember what Dad told us?" she said, suddenly. "The Shamash is the servant candle because it lights all the others. Remember, Gidon, that's what Dad said. We should be like servant candles. Dad said it's better to be a servant than a hero."

Little Amos, who was four and already in his pajamas, had fallen asleep as they talked. Galit carefully picked him up, carried him into his room, and gently slipped him into his own little bed.

After that, the two went on talking until bedtime. But once in bed, they couldn't sleep. Maybe their tummies were too stuffed with *latkes* and sour cream, but more likely, it was because of all the thoughts going around in their heads.

The more Gidon thought about living in the days of the Maccabees, the more it seemed like a great adventure. After lying awake for a long time, Gidon crept quietly into Galit's room to see if she was still awake.

"Galit!" he whispered, "Are you sleeping?"

"No, I can't sleep," she murmured. "Keep thinking

11

about the Maccabees."

"You too?"

"Yes. Did you ever stop to think that Modi'in, the village where it all started, is just a few miles from here?"

"I know. Except for all the years that have passed, we could have been part of it."

"Uh-huh. But it was a lon-n-ng time back and we still have school tomorrow. We'd better go to bed, Gidon," she mumbled sleepily.

"No! I can't sleep, Galit! I wish we could put on some magic rings or something and zoom back to that time."

"Zoom back to the time of the Maccabees?"

"Yeah!"

"Maybe," Galit mumbled back dreamily. "But I wouldn't want to be stuck there."

"Galit, get up! I'm going to the living room to have a look at Dad's dreidles. Come on! We're not going to sleep anyway."

"Haven't you looked at those dreidles enough times?"

"I don't care. I have a hunch there's something special there. I want to see them again," he insisted, tugging at his sister and bringing her, shuffling along halfheartedly behind him.

The large living room was filled with shadows at this hour. It was no use turning on a light and rousing their parents who always kept their door slightly ajar at night. The two tiptoed silently to the far corner of the room where an imposing mahogany cabinet stood with ornately carved wooden doors. Fortunately, the cupboard had a little light of its own which switched on from the inside when the doors were opened.

"What do you want to do here, Gidon?" Galit asked crossly again, still feeling drawn back to her own cozy bed.

"I just want to spin that one dreidle again," Gidon insisted, looking over the items in the cabinet. "I love seeing how the colors all melt into a rainbow when they whirl."

"It is lovely to watch," Galit agreed.

The light shed its faint rays on a wide assortment of knickknacks collected over the years. There were tiny animals in glass, small statues, ivory inlaid pill boxes and countless treasures. The children loved to look through everything, only looking of course, as they were forbidden to touch most of the mementos. But with the dreidles, spinning was allowed. They just had to be spun in the center of the dining table or on the floor, where they wouldn't hit a fragile ornament.

Reaching his hand onto the lower shelf which held the dreidles, Gidon picked up what he thought was his favorite and laid it on the table.

"Gidon, that's not a dreidle! What did you pick up?"

"It's some kind of a block with a funny curved bottom. I thought it was a dreidle. I never noticed it before."

"Let me look at it a minute. This curved bottom is really weird. It's like a rocker. And it's got – let's see , two, three, four, six sides! And these letters – they're probably Greek. I wonder what it says?"

"You're right, they must be Greek," Gidon agreed, not really knowing what Greek letters looked like. "But the letters aren't only in Greek. Look! Under each big letter someone has written a smaller one in Hebrew!"

"Put it on the table! I want to see what it spells."

"It's easy. *Koof - resh - vav - nun - vav - samech.*"

"That spells CRONOS. It can't be anything else."

"But what's CRONOS?"

"It's not 'what?'" Galit corrected. "It's who? I think it's the name of a Greek god."

"A Greek god? What do we have that in our house for?"

"Don't be silly, Gidon! It's not the god itself. It's just the name."

"Still, it makes me feel weird. We've just seen that movie about the troubles in the days of the Maccabees because our people worshipped Greek gods."

"I know. The Jews were divided: Some wanted to worship according to the Torah, and some just forgot the God of Israel."

"Maybe CRONOS is just the name of a Greek word?" Gidon asked hopefully.

"Could be. Maybe the Greek word for Time, though I thought CRONOS was the god of Time."

"Galit, look at that block! Do you see what it's doing? Did you start it rocking when you laid it down?"

"No, I didn't."

"Well, it's rocking now. It's clicking all over the place. I don't like it."

"Put it back in the cupboard, Gidon. You shouldn't have touched it."

"I know, and I sure don't want to touch it again."

"Okay, I'll put it back then," Galit offered gallantly. Then she added, a little nervously, "You just hold onto me in case it does something unusual."

"I'm holding you. Okay, go ahead!"

When the two children picked up the rocking CRONOS block something unusual did happen. It was something so strange and remarkable, in fact, that the children were never able to explain it.

THE TRAITOR

At first, the children began rocking back and forth, shaking, just like the CRONOS block itself. Then they felt themselves moving – floating – lifting – virtually sailing through the air, through the walls, through the inky black night and out to an open, bright space. There, strangest of all, the clouds were flying backwards and the children seemed to be flying backwards, as well. They were moving, not only through space but also through time, and all the while the CRONOS block that Galit was still holding, was ticking, ticking, ticking – not minutes nor hours but years and centuries! They were swirling and whirling in the midst of it all – almost dancing at times, backwards through endless space and time.

When all the flurry and the whirling came to a stop at last, both children felt a gentle thud as their feet touched down. They were standing in a place where they'd never been before – in a large market square. It was good that both Galit and Gidon were together in this very strange place. But where were they? The mood was heavy. Solemn, in fact. Many people were gathered in the square. They looked sad and worried. Some were draped in dark cloaks reaching to their ankles. Many were wearing nothing but old, brown sacks. The children, looking down at themselves, found they were now fully dressed. Miraculously, instead of pajamas, they were wearing brown outfits not unlike those of the people

They were swirling and whirling in
the midst of it all.

around them. Galit found she had a large, convenient pocket on the side of her skirt and quickly slipped the CRONOS block into the pocket. Gidon for his part had already forgotten about it. They were soon both fully absorbed in the wonder of what was taking place.

The people stood scattered in front of a crude altar built of rocks and stones and no one was speaking. It was as though no one dared make a sound.

Still in a daze, Galit and Gidon stood there, riveted to the ground, taking it all in. Then Gidon looked around uncertainly, hardly daring to breathe or move. There was terrible tension in the air. Suddenly, the screeching of an animal startled them, shaking the two out of their daze. Their eyes raced toward the sound of the piercing squeal where they saw a dirty pig tied with heavy rope to some rocks. The pig was squirming and tugging, trying to break loose. Galit almost laughed at the funny sight, but caught herself.

"Look, Gidon! Look at the pig!" she whispered.

"I am!" Her brother answered. "What's that pig doing here?"

"Don't know. I don't know what anybody is doing here. It scares me. Notice how sad they look?" she answered under her breath.

"And how worried!" he added.

The children were partly hidden from view by the crowd – perhaps because they were smaller than most of the people standing there. No one noticed them. It was as though they were invisible.

To one side of the rocky altar stood three lines of fierce-looking men. They were soldiers, all wearing similar tunics. Each held an old-fashioned spear or sword of some sort and a helmet on his head. Before them, lounging on a strange, portable cot, was a scowling, arrogant man with plump, sagging cheeks. Strapped to his side was a brass-gilded sword. He was clearly the one everyone feared.

The soldiers and their commander stood to the left of the altar of rocks. To its right stood five robust, broad-shouldered men. These five, who were dressed much like the other villagers, didn't seem as worried as everyone else. There was something different about them. Beside them was an old man with a flowing beard and a long white robe. He looked like an old rabbi.

"Gidon, what does that pig make you think of?" Galit whispered.

"I don't know. Can't think of anything except the pig the people of Modi'in were supposed to kill to please the Greeks."

"To please the Greeks? That's what it is, Gidon!" she said, her eyes growing big. Quickly clapping a finger over her lips, she whispered excitedly, "It's *the* pig!"

As the children watched, the commander with the glimmering sword rose to his feet. At once, the foot soldiers snapped their heels to attention and stood very straight. Then the commander strode straight out in front of the Altar, turned to the crowd, and shouted, "Men of Judea, today you will sacrifice to the great god, Zeus! These are orders from the King!"

Turning to the elderly man in the white gown, he said, "You, Mattityahu Maccabee, are priest and leader here. You must sacrifice first!"

The children looked, wide eyed. So this *was* Modi'in! This was the days of the Maccabees! A thrill of recognition ran through them. But it lasted only seconds. The next minute they were gripped by the horror of what was happening.

"Come forward, and offer this noble beast, Maccabee!" the commander commanded. "Set an example for your townsmen! Be the first honored man to taste the sacred flesh. Silver and gold will be yours and the King will call you friend!"

The children held their breath. What would happen? Would he do it? They both began to tremble.

When the commander saw the old priest refusing to move forward, he became angry, "What other leaders have done in Judea's other towns, you must do here. Your people obey the King everywhere. In Jerusalem, too, they have offered a pig."

The children looked at each other. In a flash, Galit recalled from the Hanukkah movie how Jews who disobeyed were hurled over high walls by the Greeks. No, by the Seleucids! – which was the part of the Greek army which ruled in Judea. They had punished those Jews who kept Moses' teachings and they made unclean all that was holy in the glorious Temple in Jerusalem. For a faithful Jew this was the worst thing that could happen.

Galit and Gidon were watching the old priest. The commander changed tactics and was speaking softly to the venerable old sage.

"Just look at him! He's trying to trick Mattityahu Maccabee!" Galit whispered and they both nodded.

The children could see a fierce, angry glare come into the old priest's eyes. That determined look promised he would not be swayed – not for honors, not for gold, not for anything. They shuddered, thinking of all that could happen to him if he didn't obey.

Mattityahu stepped forward, head high, shoulders firm. In a booming voice he cried, "Though all the people in the King's empire worship the gods of the Greeks, I and my sons will *never* do it. We will not obey the foul laws of the King nor turn from our sacred laws!"

"Galit, something terrible is about to happen," Gidon whispered to his sister.

"We know what it is. There'll be a fight!" she whispered back. "He's so brave! He knows that nobody can defy King Epiphanes and stay alive! "

"I wish everyone in the village were as brave as Mattityahu," Gidon sighed.

"So do I."

"Wait! Look! What's happening?"

A Judean villager was stepping forward – a single, sorrowful man with a tattered cloak. He was not defiant like the old priest. He walked bent-over and looked defeated. Without glancing around, he went right to the altar where the commander stood. Everyone was watching him tensely.

"Give me that pig, sir!" he said. "I'll do the job." Then he mumbled under his breath, "Somebody has to or we'll all die!"

A few villagers sighed. The soldiers seemed relieved. They wouldn't have to start a fight after all.

The villager was about to offer the pig. Holding it down with one hand, he raised his sword with the other. The commander looked pleased and nodded his head. The soldiers enjoyed what was happening.

"You traitor!" The old priest cried loudly. "You will betray us!"

"You traitor!" the old priest cried loudly.
"You will betray us!"

Before anyone knew it, Mattityahu Maccabee lunged forward, snatched the man's gleaming sword, and struck him. The Judean man crumbled to the ground. The next moment, not the pig but the villager lay dead in a pool of blood.

As though awakened from a deep sleep, the villagers suddenly flew into action. Pandemonium broke loose. The five strong men behind Mattityahu began wrenching swords and spears out of the hands of soldier after soldier. They fell upon the commander. The other villagers, too, hurled themselves upon the soldiers. Using their fists, sturdy sticks – whatever they could find – they pounded the soldiers. In an instant, those sullen, quiet villagers became fierce warriors. They attacked the soldiers with the same powerful strokes the old priest had used on the traitor. It was a horrible sight for Gidon and Galit to see.

Yet, what seemed like an unending battle, was finished in a few minutes. As quickly as the fighting started, it was over, and quiet returned. The children looked around and saw the entire unit of soldiers as well as their mighty commander, lying dead on the ground.

QUIET AFTER THE STORM

Not only Gidon and Galit but everyone in Modi'in was shaken by what happened. Even the old priest and his sons were trembling. They were all astonished. They doubted whether any among them – men, women or children – would be alive by the end of that day. Yet, here they all stood. The sun was high in the sky and their would-be killers were dead. It had all happened so fast.

The people in Modi'in were not used to fighting. Most of the men were farmers. They cared for their families, their homes, their flocks. In the springtime they planted their seed. When the fruit and grain were ripe, they harvested their crops. Their lives had a quiet rhythm – work six days and rest on the seventh. But these were not usual times. Ever since the cruel Epiphanes became king, everything had changed. Every day they heard news of people being tortured, terrorized and put to death. Many ran to hide in desert caves. Nobody dared to fight back.

Galit and Gidon were pale as ghosts. They had seen everything. Yet, nobody seemed to notice they were there. Strangely, they had not been seen. But now a small boy hiding in his mother's skirts, peeped out at them and screamed,

"Who are you? You don't belong here! Go away!"

His mother, dressed in a homespun tunic, glanced around but didn't see them.

"Hush!" she said.

The five men, who resembled each other so much they had to be brothers, were standing with the white-bearded priest and speaking in low tones, their faces white as sheets.

But what *were* they saying? The children strained to catch each word. They heard only bits and pieces.

"...do now?...a blow...more than hoped...ready to die...we must rally...fight back...stay alive...will strike again...regain the Temple...God be..."

The children were not sure how to piece it all together. But from what they heard they were sure of one thing. The bloodshed was not over. There would be more.

A few minutes passed and the five men walked to one side. After that, the children couldn't catch any more words, not until the old priest stepped forward and spoke to everyone. In a trembling voice he said:

"Men and women of Modi'in, our lives have been spared by the providence of God. He gave us victory. This is a sign that God is with us! He will win back for us all we have lost. Freedom will return to our land. We will worship again as we were taught. The glorious Temple will be restored. But friends and villagers, it will be hard. Some will not live to see it. Freedom will be dearly bought."

At this, the brawniest of the five men, Judah, came forward to address the people.

"Listen carefully," he said. "We must flee our village. None of us will be safe here. He who would stand up for the Laws of our God must abandon his home and his fields. The King will send new legions to destroy us. We must take to the hills. Every man and every family, make ready! We depart at sundown! Let no man stay behind!"

After these solemn words, the whole village was choked with fear – everyone was afraid to forsake all they had, afraid of what lay ahead and afraid to stay behind. Yet, as they talked among themselves, a spark of hope was lit and its fire raced from heart to heart. People began moving, hurrying to do whatever they must.

The small boy who had seen Galit and Gidon earlier, now pointed to them again, "Not them! They're not coming," he screamed. "You two, go away!"

This time the brawny man, Judah, who had taken command, came and took a long look at Galit and Gidon.

"Who are you?" he demanded.

Gidon, to his own amazement, was quick to answer. "We're Jews. My name is Gidon, I'm a good runner. My sister, Galit, is great with a slingshot. We want to stand with you!"

Galit looked at Gidon with horror but also a touch of excitement.

"What are you saying, Gidon? Speak for yourself!"

Ignoring his sister, Gidon went on loudly, "Please let us come! I know we can help!"

Judah looked uncertainly at the two children, mystified and unsure. Then he said in a harried tone, "I don't know where you two came from, but you may be useful. If you can handle the hardships, come along."

After that Judah forgot about them and continued preparing everyone for their flight, telling the townspeople what to bring along and what to leave behind.

A HARROWING HIKE

That very evening, Gidon and Galit, together with the villagers who gathered their bundles, their animals and their children, made ready to depart. As the great gold coin of the sun dropped into its slot behind rose-colored clouds, the rowdy and boisterous crew set off on its way.

The spell of dread among the villagers had broken. The crowd was very noisy. People were chattering and clattering everywhere. The babbling of countless voices was only interrupted by the occasional wailing of a child or the deep-throated orders of the old priest.

"You men, get over here! The stronger ones in Simon's group! Heave these bundles! Move that cart!

"Older women and little ones, go to Jonathan farther on!

"Eleazar's group, bring up the rear! You two children! Newcomers! Eleazar's group for you!"

Mattityahu Maccabee was organizing them all. The people fell in line in five bands, each led by one of the brothers. Along with them were sheep and goats. There were donkeys loaded with grain, dried fruit and farming tools. Some donkeys were pulling carts. Galit and Gidon had been put in a group with mostly women and children.

"This isn't for me!" Gidon objected loudly. "I want to be in front with the men!"

"Shhh Gidon! Quiet!" Galit scolded. "If you fuss, Judah Maccabee will say we can't come. I don't want to stay in Modi'in. Do you? The King's soldiers would finish us off in a hurry."

"You're right about that. That's the last thing I want. But this group is too slow."

"I know, Gidon. We could both go a lot faster. Remember the camping trip we took to the mountains of Gophna? That was a four-hour hike. This way it'll take all night. But we didn't have all this heavy stuff to carry when we did it with the sports team."

"Or all these animals to drag along."

"Strange the way the people talk, isn't it?" Galit remarked. "I don't understand what they're saying half the time. Their Hebrew is really different from ours!"

As they moved along, listening, intrigued, they strained to make out what the people near them were saying. All at once a boy about Gidon's age darted in front of them.

"What's this cutting into the line?" Gidon cried out heatedly. "Watch where you're going!"

The boy whirled around and his mouth dropped open. He was surprised by this strange boy whose words he could barely make out. Yet, Gidon's anger had come across and the boy's face showed dismay. Now the boy was looking straight at him, and Gidon saw his face for the first time. At once he felt sick. The boy was in a bad way. His eyes were puffy and red, what you could see of them. The left one was swollen shut. Over his cheek was a purplish blue welt. His cloak was also torn.

Gidon felt terrible about the way he had spoken. "I'm sorry," he blurted. "I-I-I didn't know."

"Didn't know? Didn't know what?! I don't know what you said, but I don't like it! Where did you come from?" he went on and, seeing Galit, added, "You're not from here either!"

In spite of his puffed eyes and miserable looks, Gidon was getting a good feeling about this boy. He was spunky. *I'm going to tell him what we're here for*, he thought. *We might win a friend. That's worth a lot.*

"I'm Gidon Rosen. This is Galit. My sister and I come from Tel Aviv."

"Tel-a-what?"

"Tel Aviv. You've never heard of it. It's in a whole other world. We're from centuries after your days, but we're Jews and we're proud of it! We want to join you and fight for the honor of God!"

"Another world? Another time? How can that be?"

"We don't know, but here we are." The children were too perplexed to even try to explain.

"Hum," the boy was thoughtful. "You don't know how you got here but you want to help us. We could sure use help from another world – we need all the help we can get. What time is it now in your world?"

"About the same time as here, only years and years later."

"Years later? How many?"

"Wait a minute and I'll tell you."

"Gidon isn't good at doing sums," Galit spoke up for her brother. "Our time is nearly two thousand and two hundred years later than in your days."

"What? You want me to believe that? Why would anyone go that far BACKWARDS in time to be with us in our days? You've gone all those years BACKWARDS just to help us?"

"That's right," Gidon answered.

"How do you know it's that many years?" the boy asked.

"We've read about you in our history books."

"Yes, and you're going to win, too. That's also in the books." Galit added. "Just don't give up. That's the main thing. Don't give up!"

"We won't do that!" Through his puffy eyes and bruised face, the boy beamed a broad smile. "God is helping us. We wouldn't risk our homes and everything if we didn't believe that."

"It's a lot to give up," Galit agreed.

"It'll be good to have you two along. I'm Eliram," the boy smiled again. "But what's that you said?" he went on. "About *histree bucks*? What are they?"

Gidon and Galit were puzzled. Then all at once Galit caught on. "You mean our history books, don't you? You've never seen a book, I suppose. You have scrolls but we have books. History books are like scrolls. They have a lot of pages with writing on them. They tell stories of things that really happened."

"Hmm... Interesting. Do the stories have happy endings?"

"Well, uh, some of them. The one about *your* battles does."

"Thanks for saying that!"

"Eliram, excuse me. Do you mind if I ask you something?" Gidon wondered. "What happened to your face?"

"You can see it?" Eliram looked disappointed.

"Sure can."

"I got into a fight. It wasn't my fault. This fellow,

Julius, kept bullying me. He started punching and wouldn't stop. I got angry and beat him up. He's a Judean, but not like us. You know what I mean?"

"Not really."

"Not all Jews see things like we do. This boy likes Greek customs and sports and all that – everything the invaders like. He even likes their gods!"

"So what caused the fight?"

"He was boasting about all his father's Greek coins. Finally, I couldn't take it. I took a beating, but I got the better of him!" Eliram concluded, beaming.

"Is this boy from Modi'in?"

"What do you think? If he and his father had been there, things wouldn't have gone the way they did. Julius' father would have offered the pig for sure to their *beloved* Zeus. His friends would have helped him. Even the old priest couldn't have stopped them. They've betrayed our people before."

"That's terrible! I see why you're angry!" Gidon said sympathetically.

"Hush! Look! There to the right! What do you see?" Eliram asked, pointing.

"Torches in the valley!" Gidon exclaimed.

"It sure looks like it! They're coming this way. Quick, let's run to our leaders and warn them!"

"If it's a Seleucid patrol, we're done for!" Gidon called out, already running.

"I'm with you, Gidon!" cried Eliram.

The boys set off at their fastest pace. Both found it rough going. Gidon kept stubbing his feet on roots and rocks as they sped past one side of the crowd. Bits of gravel ground between their toes. Gidon's heart was pounding as he breathed a prayer to God and lunged forward catching his foot behind a rock. He freed himself and continued to press on. Then he suddenly noticed he was bounding and gliding right over rocks and bushes. The scrubby undergrowth no longer threatened him as he flew past in a flurry and a blurr.

He looked to see if Eliram was there, but couldn't make him out. The next minute, Gidon found himself standing, puffing and panting, right in front of Judah Maccabee at the beginning of the line.

"Judah Maccabee, it's me, Gidon! We've spotted danger. Eliram came, too. Eliram, where are you?!" He looked about frantically, but couldn't find his new friend.

"So what's your warning, my boy?" Judah asked.

"There were torches in the valley."

At that moment Eliram came up, panting. "A patrol's spotted us from the rear, Judah Maccabee," he said, breathing heavily. "If we're going to get away from them, we have to act fast!"

The big, hulking man gave the boys a brief look and nodded approvingly, "You two boys have got your senses about you. Here in the front we haven't seen any patrols. You were quick to sight danger."

Then, throwing his thickly-bearded head back, he gazed into the heavens.

"Protector of Israel," he cried, "lay Your mighty hand on our people this night. Shield us for Your great Name's sake and for Your holy Temple!" His words vibrated and filled the air like a booming bassoon. Gidon shuddered. Even the ground trembled beneath them.

Whether or not the patrols see us, they will surely hear us, Gidon thought, as Judah's prayers broke the stillness of night. Yet, the power in that prayer was strangely uplifting.

He looked around to see how Eliram had taken it. Surely, he was shaken, as well? What he saw unsettled him even more than the loud booming prayer. He saw – or rather, he didn't see – anything! Only a thick, cloudy whiteness before his face. A fog had enveloped them so quickly, he didn't know where it came from. The face of his new friend, Eliram, had disappeared. The air was so cloudy and so heavy with blinding mist, he saw no faces at all.

GALIT'S TRIUMPH

A great cloud descending upon them had hidden all from view. Suddenly, each person could only see a few steps ahead. Nothing else was visible for the first few moments. People were calling out in muffled voices to find each other. They were disoriented. Yet, the plodding continued. Everyone, from the oldest to the youngest, knew they must keep up the march no matter what. They continued what had become a steady upward climb.

Galit had just noticed her brother was not behind her when the fog closed in. There were reasons why she didn't miss him sooner. Much had been happening at her end of the line. First, there was the frightening incident with the small child. Galit had noticed this beady-eyed, black-haired wisp of a little girl hanging over the side of a donkey cart just ahead, reaching for some toy of hers that had fallen. As Galit watched, she saw the child slip and, suddenly, there she was dangling over the side. Galit made a wild dash for her and managed to grab the little girl just as her shiny black locks began tangling themselves into the large wooden wheel. When people realized what was happening they began screaming and shouting. First the cart and then all of Eleazer's group came to a halt. One of the men flew into action trying to unwind the frightened child's tangled hair. A woman tried to calm the little girl, while someone else took a sharp knife and cut her loose from the wooden wheel. Women were crowding around and the child was

...her shiny black locks began tangling
themselves into the large wooden wheel.

screaming loudly. Galit heard them calling her Becca.

"Becca, *Chamuda*! It will grow back!" someone was saying.

Becca wasn't badly hurt, only beside herself for the shiny locks she'd lost. When all the commotion died down, the women turned to Galit. They began patting, hugging and squeezing the breath out of her with their warm bodies.

"Who are you? Where did you come from? Why have you come along?" they asked. Galit was at a loss to find answers.

To make matters worse, a tall, lanky man with bushy, black locks hanging over his brow, suddenly pushed the women aside, shouting, "Where is the girl who rescued Becca?" His voice made Galit tremble. Would he and the others say she and Gidon shouldn't have come along? The next moment, standing before him and seeing the gentle light in this man's eyes, Galit saw she had nothing to fear.

"Here, my girl," he said. "Take this! You acted quickly to save our child. You were brave. This is a token of our thanks."

It was an odd-shaped thing the man placed in her hand. Galit didn't take time to look at it carefully. In the midst of all the excitement she simply closed her hand tightly around the object and placed it in her satchel.

"She's a guardian angel come to help us!" one woman exclaimed. Others were speaking more words of praise.

An angel? What an idea! Poor Galit, who never liked being fussed over, felt a red blush rise in her face.

Only when everyone in Galit's group returned to

their normal plodding, did Galit look around for Gidon. Nor did she have much time. The next thing she knew the cloud had come down over her as it came over them all. It served as a protection – an answer to Judah's mighty prayer. But Galit didn't know this. Nor did the others. All they knew was you couldn't see five feet in front of you. It was hard not to stumble on boulders and branches or whatever lay across the path.

Galit began to panic and called loudly through the fog to her brother, but got no answer.

Then the group slowed down and came to a standstill. Words were passed from man to man. A patrol had been spotted and they were to wait till it passed.

People gathered in small bunches, talking in low tones. Galit reached into her satchel to look at the gift from Becca's father. She pulled out a y-shaped stick, beautifully carved, with a looped strap extended between the prongs.

"It's a slingshot!" she said. "What a gift! I'm sure going to make use of this!"

She had stopped worrying about Gidon. He could take care of himself. He was probably off with some of the men.

PITCHING CAMP

When the fog lifted, the plodding began again at a slow, wearisome pace. It was some time later Judah Maccabee finally announced they had reached their woodland hideout and the tired trekkers laid down their loads in exhausted relief. The first rays of dawn were already stealing through the heavy clouds in the eastern sky. Galit collapsed in a heap on a small mound of grass without further thought. Her aching legs had been saying, "No more!" for hours. She hardly cared where she landed. In a few minutes she was sound asleep.

Gidon and Eliram were still at the head of the line, close on the heels of Judah and the old priest. They found a resting spot together. Eliram spread out his large cloak on the ground and it was big enough for them both. No sooner had the two exhausted boys stretched out and laid down, than they too, were deep in slumber.

None of the three children so much as stirred until the sun was high in the sky. When Galit rubbed her eyes and looked around, she couldn't grasp what she saw. Where was her own white-painted desk and comfortable wicker chair? Where were all the familiar stuffed animals that usually greeted her when she awoke? Now, instead, she saw a steep, bare, rocky slope and an open grassy stretch closed in on three sides. Tall trees and scrubby bushes surrounded the wide space. On the fourth side was the sheer drop of a cliff opening onto a wide valley.

As she looked around, Galit noticed groups of

people standing in plain, dingy tunics, tending small fires. Large jars were steaming, hanging between two poles. There were families squatting and eating out of crockery jars. Children were running about screaming or playing some sort of tag. And there was that beady-eyed little Becca. A few black ringlets were missing from one side of her head. This was the same child whose lovely curls had been crudely chopped off when she tumbled from the cart.

With that the whole picture came back. Galit had made it to camp, too tired to check out the ground beneath her, before falling asleep. A sense of excitement came over her again – the same zest for adventure she had felt the day before, when Gidon urged Judah Maccabee to let them come along. But what would happen now? Would they survive? Enemy soldiers could discover their hiding place any time. Surely the soldiers would find them – but how long would it take? And how would they ever escape?

And Gidon? What happened to him? She must try to find Gidon!

At the far end of the camp he and Eliram were also starting to stir. The first thing Gidon noticed when he awoke was Judah pacing back and forth at the edge of the clearing.

"Eliram, what do you make of Judah Maccabee? What's he doing?"

"He's probably thinking and figuring out what we'll do next," said Eliram, yawning and stretching his long, skinny arms.

"Not Judah. He's already decided," Gidon said admiringly.

"You're probably right. Maybe he's pacing out lookout posts at the crest of the hill, overlooking the valley. Look, Gidon! He's choosing men to stand guard!"

Gidon was all eyes. He was ready to run out and offer to stand guard at once. But then he realized the awful gnawing in his stomach and thought better of it. When had he eaten last? He couldn't remember. He *had* to have something to eat! And then, where was Galit? Where was she? Gidon was a little worried. Should he try to find Galit at once or first get something to eat?

He decided first he must eat!

THE VIGIL

Gidon and Eliram quickly found Galit after they had eaten that morning. The people were spread out, but there wasn't much space to get lost in their tiny camping ground. Galit had been searching for them as well and the three were glad to find each other. They had much to tell about what they'd been doing.

The next few days were filled with hour upon hour of waiting and watching for even the smallest platoon of soldiers. That's all it would take to overrun the weary campers.

Gidon and Eliram were posted for nightly vigils at likely ambush spots. Galit, known to her friends as a skilled marksman, stood guard duty at the crest of the cliff. Time for sleeping was scarce. Food rations were growing less each day.

Everyone knew that something had to be done so the food wouldn't run out. Judah Maccabee, Eleazer, Jonathan, Simon and Yochanan, the five brothers, were organizing guerrilla training drills and mustering up the able-bodied men. But when you're hungry it's hard to train for battle. And they weren't an army yet – just a gangling group of Judean farmers with pickaxes and pitchforks. They had the spirit needed to drive the enemy back, but nobody had much faith in their untested guerrilla tactics. The King's army could find them any day, any moment.

But even if they weren't discovered, what then?

How long could their little band last? Everyone had questions and no answers. All that was certain was, they had to have food!

About halfway through the first week Judah and the old priest gathered the people together to explain things. They needed to forge links with nearby villagers – with loyal Judeans who could make up a backup force and a food supply line from the farms. Messengers would be chosen to leave the camp and scout for friendly farmers, who could share food from their crops. They would also look for men to join their drills and beef up their ranks.

When the people heard this, excitement spread through the camp. Who would be sent? If things went wrong and the messengers got caught, they would be killed. If the wrong messengers were sent, they might desert. There was so much at stake. Everything would depend on the messengers getting through safely and finding the right people. Many Judean villagers had chosen to side with the Greeks and might well turn them in for a reward.

When Mattityahu Maccabee finished speaking he said, "Fear not, my people. Let us pray and take courage! The God of Israel is with us!"

"I'd sure like to be one of those first scouts," Gidon whispered to Eliram. "I know where I'd go and what I'd do!" he went on, boastfully.

"Listen to him talk," Eliram answered, casting a knowing look at Galit. "Gidon, you've already forgotten how I got roughed up the day everything happened in Modi'in. Don't forget, all our Jewish brothers aren't friends. Some are worse than enemies!"

"I haven't forgotten. I still want to go. I'm not afraid to die if I have to," he whispered.

"Gidon, you don't understand," Galit broke in impatiently. "Living can be harder than dying. Our job is to keep vigil at our posts. That's the best thing we can do right now. Remember what Judah told us when he gave us our guard posts? If it gets boring – and it sure does! – we have to think of why we are here. If the enemy takes us by surprise, it won't be boring!"

Judah Maccabee was talking. They were still too few people to stage a revolt. They needed more men. Enemy soldiers were everywhere. Judean supporters could bring them reports on where soldiers were patrolling. Men at the base needed to know when enemy patrols were coming their way. Besides, Judah's men needed weapons. Above all, what they needed most now was food.

"I wish I would be chosen," Gidon sighed again. "I'd sure like to be one of those first scouts."

ELEPHANT ENCOUNTER

They were in limbo with no sign of the enemy. The silence was eery. Not a twig crunched nor a distant horn rumbled. Neither the muffled clatter of wagon wheels far off nor the jangle of steel blades on armor were heard. And so it had been now for days.

Gidon, Galit and Eliram had all come to the end of their nightly vigils. Galit and Gidon crept into the woolly sheep hides each had been given, to catch some sleep for the last hours of night. Eliram settled himself beside them, bundled in his cloak,

Though it was late, the three began to talk.

"Strange, the Governor's men haven't spotted us!" Galit began.

"It's five days since the soldiers were killed at Modi'in," Eliram commented.

"The Judean Governor has to be furious that we killed his commander," Galit went on.

"Angry and embarrassed," Eliram added. "You're right, Galit. Still, he probably doesn't want anyone to know he lost a commander and all those men. I've a hunch he may not even chase us."

"He may not chase us? What about the patrol we spotted?" Gidon roused himself from his dozing.

"They were just doing their job. For all we know they never saw us," Eliram thought aloud.

"Eliram, why wouldn't the Governor chase us? He doesn't want us to start a revolt."

"A revolt, Gidon?" said Galit. "You've got your history mixed. No one would ever have dreamed of a revolt by a bunch of simple farmers in these days! The Greeks aren't afraid of us. They probably think we'll all die of starvation or give ourselves up. They don't know we have a God who fights our battles!"

They all nodded. With heavy eyelids, they settled down atop their rocky beds and were soon sleeping.

It wasn't much later that Galit was awakened by the distant sounds of rumbling and trumpeting.

"Gidon, wake up!" she whispered, shaking him hard. "I hear something and it keeps getting louder!"

"Huh? Where? Let me sleep!" he mumbled.

"There in the valley! Something's going on! We've got to check it out!" she insisted, urgently, half-dragging Gidon to a lookout post at the top of the cliff. By this time Gidon was wide awake and what met the eyes of the two children astounded them both. In the faint morning light, lumbering along at a gradual pace, were huge elephants, each with four or five soldiers mounted on their backs.

"Look! There're two of them! Three! Four!"

"And they're still coming!"

"Now they're passing at the foot of the cliff!"

"I can't believe they haven't spotted our camp!"

"Maybe they have and they're looking for a path to climb up!"

"They won't find a path wide enough for the elephants!"

"Shhh! Hide behind these shrubs! They mustn't see us!" Galit cautioned.

"Galit! Come on! Let's get down there! I want to

have a better look!"

"That's not a good idea. What if they see us?"

"We won't let them!" Gidon had already begun scrambling down the steep slope into the valley. Galit was disturbed by her brother's persistence but still followed him halfheartedly.

By the time the two reached the roadway at the base of the cliff, the elephant caravan had already gone on.

"Now, you see! We missed them, anyway!" Galit scolded.

"No we haven't! I've got an idea," Gidon answered.

"What's that?"

"That roadway loops back as it goes down along the slope."

"Sooo?"

"If we can cut straight down through here, we'll meet them where the road comes back."

"Lead on! I still can't believe they haven't noticed our camp. "

"They don't even suspect it! They didn't slow down! Let's go down this way where it's clear of bushes."

"Watch out for those rocks! They could come crashing down!" Galit warned, but her warning was too late. Gidon had already set his foot on an unsteady rock at the same moment that it started rolling.

"Help! I'm falling, Galit!" he cried frantically.

"I've got you!" she rushed to respond, grasping his hand, but her own foothold wasn't steady either and before they knew it, they were both sliding down the slope in an avalanche of stones and pebbles and rocks.

They kept slipping and skidding and couldn't grab hold of anything, until finally, they landed right in the path of the oncoming elephants, without even a moment to scramble to their feet.

"Get up and run, Gidon!" Galit cried.

"I can't! We won't make it in time! We'll get squashed!"

"God, help us!" Galit prayed desperately.

As they looked up, a mammoth elephant foot was coming down on them both. It crashed to the ground, barely missing the children. The next thing they knew they were being raised high in the air in the crook of the elephant's trunk – so high they could see the soldiers mounted on its huge back, with their swords and javelins pointing straight toward them.

"Help!" Galit cried again.

The elephant kept swinging them back and forth and up and down, never loosening his grip, until the children were sick with dizziness and full of fear they would be tossed onto the elephant's back where the soldiers would quickly finish them off. His trunk was squeezing them so tightly they could barely breathe.

Then, as quickly as he'd picked them up, the elephant loosened his grip and laid them down gingerly by the side of the road. The children crouched where they landed, amazed, gasping and incredulous at the miracle that had saved their lives. They watched the huge elephant slowly return to his lumbering pace in the caravan. They didn't even dare move until the whole elephant patrol had disappeared well out of sight. Only then could they breathe easily and begin checking their bruised arms and legs to make sure they were all right.

His trunk was squeezing them so tightly
they could barely breathe.

LAUNCHING OUT

Though the two children were very bruised and sore when they finally made it back up the steep slope to the camp, they were full of excitement, eager to report on what they'd seen.

"Eliram, you won't believe what happened to us in the valley!" Gidon boasted, as he described in detail their harrowing ordeal.

When, a little later they reported to Judah, he was interested in learning more about the armed elephant patrol. Yet, the children were severely scolded for running off on their own without alerting him.

A few days later, the first team was selected to launch out and search for villagers friendly to their cause. Everybody expected Judah and one of his brothers to make the expedition alone. To the surprise of all, Judah and Eleazer asked all three children and two more men to be part of the group.

"You boys are good runners," said Judah Maccabee. "You can be helpful once you learn to recognize Judeans who are loyal. Come with us! This will be good training. And you, Galit, are a quick-witted girl. You will pick up strategic information which the boys can relay back to the base.

"But everyone must follow orders. That is rule number one!" Judah announced.

The children were beside themselves with joy. They were being entrusted with important work! Little did they know the trouble that lay ahead.

The first rays of dawn were breaking as the four men and three children emerged from the forest. They had walked for hours, scrambling over brush and rocky inclines, through brambles and thickets. The children didn't have an easy time keeping up with the broad strides of Judah and Eleazer. With the coming of dawn, the pleasant chirping and twittering of birds emerged from the trees and bushes.

"The birds sing so cheerfully. They haven't a thought about the harsh invaders controlling their woods," said Eleazer and sighed. The children stopped a moment to listen to the twitter, then looked around anxiously.

Judah and Eleazer paused as they approached the edge of a clearing. A tiny village was snuggled into the valley below. A whole cluster of white, flat-top houses could be seen beneath them, scattered among colorful gardens.

"There it is, – *Zichron Moshe*," announced Judah. "It's name means 'memory of Moses.' May God lead us to men who truly stand for his laws!"

It was a solemn moment. The children had grown accustomed to the dramatic way Judah spoke. Eleazer was quieter. When Eleazer did speak, you knew he would say something he had thought about for a long time.

"Brother Judah! Children! Men! We must find a spot we can clearly mark and easily find. We will all need to meet here again tomorrow at this time," Eleazer announced.

With this, they set about to find flat stones to lay in a pile beside a very large rock which stood at the edge of the clearing. This would be their meeting spot.

The plan was for them to meet in this place again at the same time the next day, and then head back to the base, together. No one would return to the base until all the scouts were accounted for. It was also agreed that no outsiders would return with them. Just the original scouts.

Gidon wondered secretly how each of them would know what "the same time tomorrow" was.

"I'm sure glad I still have my watch," he said aloud. "Too bad you took yours off when you went to bed that night before it all started happening," he added, turning to Galit.

Eliram was looking puzzled.

"A watch? What's that?"

"It's something you wear on your arm to keep track of hours and minutes," Galit explained patiently, pointing to the watch Gidon was wearing.

The three children felt reassured by the thought they would all meet again the next day. Yet, twenty-four hours can be an awfully long time, particularly if you're alone and something goes wrong.

Gidon was getting a nervous feeling in his stomach. What was lurking inside the walls of those houses down there? Were there soldiers? Were there Judeans that would betray them – men who called themselves Jews but were really the King's stooges? Where were the ones Judah wanted to find? The faithful at heart? And would they find them?

Gidon was starting to wonder why he had come along. Suddenly he didn't feel brave at all. He was tired and thirsty. His water flask had long since been drained. He was looking longingly at Galit's, still one-fourth full. Just then Galit reached for the flask and drank the last of it herself. Eliram's water was finished, too.

"All I want is to knock on that first door and get something to drink!" Gidon whispered desperately. "I don't care who answers!"

"You better care, Gidon!" Eliram countered at once. "Our lives could depend on it!"

At that very moment in one of the houses in the valley below, two soldiers were interrogating a frightened girl named Yael and a heavily-built Judean man, her father, Bar Jonah. They were trying their best to dodge the questions asked.

"Who killed the commander in Modi'in?" The soldiers demanded. "Who is the ringleader? Where is he hiding? Who overpowered our fighting men? Where are the rebels now?"

The questions were endless. Yael was confused and choked up from crying. Her father kept insisting he hadn't been in Modi'in that day.

"Believe me, I know nothing," he pleaded.

The soldiers worked together to try and trick Yael and her father. One soldier, who was broad shouldered and towered above them, seemed more gentle and sympathetic. "Tell us what you know and everything will be all right," he said.

The other soldier yelled, "We'll find out everything one way or another." He had a slithery, black mustache, catlike eyes and wiry hands.

Each time Yael's father refused to answer, this soldier would pound Bar Jonah with a heavy club and burst into a mocking laugh. "Now will you talk?!" he spat.

Then the whole process would start again.

PARTING WAYS

Meanwhile, the four men and three children had only gone a short way when Judah announced brusquely, "From this point we split up! Be strong and brave of heart! The wisdom of the Almighty will be with us!"

With this, Judah was off at a fast pace on a small trail leading east of the village. Next, Eleazer set off in another direction, his path curving around and approaching the village from behind. The other two men also strode off confidently. All four had been there in better days and knew the lay of the land. Each knew certain people they could call on.

Gidon still had a knot in his stomach. But he didn't wait long to get moving. Looking back toward the meeting spot, he took a deep breath and was on his way. He did not hear Eliram call after him, "Watch out for Julius's uncle, Gidon! The first house at the edge of town. Don't go there!"

Though they knew they, too, must take separate paths, Eliram and Galit were not as quick to part ways. Galit checked to see if her trusty slingshot was in her pouch – the gift from Becca's father, which she now used often. For the fifth time in five minutes, Eliram patted the small hand dagger he carried at his belt. Even if he wouldn't have to use it, it was good to have.

"I hope Judah and Eleazer are right about the people in this place," Galit said uncertainly.

"They are. People here love the Torah. They're

also fed up with the way we're treated by the invaders."

"But how many will risk their lives for freedom?"

"We have to find that out. I remember one neighbor of Julius' uncle who was very proud to be a Judean. That always bugged Julius. He doesn't like people like that."

"Sooo?"

"People like that neighbor might be brave enough to fight."

"Which house is theirs?"

"I wish I could remember. It's around here somewhere."

"You may remember when you get closer."

"I hope so! Watch where I go and head for the same spot. If things go well, I'll signal you to join me."

"That's a good idea, Eliram. But I'm worried about Gidon. Shouldn't we cover him? He looked very unsure of himself when he took off."

"You're right, Galit. That's another reason you should wait and come after me. One of us should hide and keep guard in case of trouble."

"I know. Someone's got to keep guard."

"Let's get going or we'll lose track of Gidon. He's only a speck on the hillside already."

THE TRAP

Gidon heard a commotion inside one of the houses when he arrived at the edge of town, but he didn't give it much thought. He was too tired, too hungry and too thirsty. He failed to listen at the door to see if it was safe to enter. Nor did he knock cautiously. Instead, he fairly banged on the door. Even the raised voices of the soldiers inside couldn't muffle that pounding.

In the house, the soldier with the catlike eyes was shaking the father, Bar Jonah, while the other jabbed him with his club. The two soldiers were forcing a confession from their miserable captives. Bar Jonah admitted he had been in Modi'in on that terrible day. He said he arrived by donkey when the sun was low. He found the place deserted with only a heap of dead bodies in the village square. But that wasn't what the soldiers wanted to hear. They wanted to know where the people of Modi'in had fled.

Bar Jonah was a short, stocky man with work-roughened hands, made hard by the plough. His coal black hair fell sideways on his brow, which was now tangled and matted with blood from the beating.

The soldier with the slithery, black mustache threatened harshly, "We have orders to kill the ringleaders. If we don't find them, we'll kill you. Tell us all you know!"

Then he shook Yael so hard that she blacked out. When her head cleared the soldier was asking her over and over, "You were there, weren't you? Who else was around? Answer me!"

At that moment Gidon banged on the door.

The minute she heard the banging, Yael felt a tremor of hope. Could this be a rescuer? A chance to escape?

No one answered and Gidon banged again. This time the pressure of the banging threw open the door! "Water! I need some water!" Gidon cried.

"Who's that boy? Grab him! " cried one of the soldiers.

The heavy-set soldier pounced on Gidon, who crumbled to the floor. Bar Jonah then threw himself on both of them. Yael, seeing her chance, made a dash for the door. She ran into the yard and from there as fast as she could toward town. The soldier with the catlike eyes took up the chase, close at her heels. Yael was light of weight and quick but no match for this lanky man. She kept running but he was closing the gap. All of a sudden there was a crrrack and a crash. Looking behind, she found her pursuer flat on the ground. She saw a sharp stone had struck him right between the eyes. The next minute a stone came whizzing past her ear. Was she being rescued or attacked? She couldn't tell. She was shaking all over and about to run again, when she heard a boy's voice from behind some shrubs,

"Galit, hold your shots. You got him. I'll take care of the girl."

Eliram and Galit emerged as from nowhere. Eliram, dagger in hand, spoke loudly to Yael, "You, girl! Stay where you are!"

"I've got to get help," Yael whimpered.

"We're here! We can help you!"

"No...stay away...I'm scared...that big brute...my father..." she said pointing to her house. "I don't want him to die!"

"Your father's in there?"

Yael nodded. "Yes. And a strange boy who wanted water."

"Her brother!" Eliram exclaimed pointing to Galit.

"Whose brother?" Yael asked, confused.

"Mine. My brother's a Jew. We all are. You can trust us. We left Modi'in to fight for freedom!"

"From Modi'in? They're after you! Better get away!"

"We're not leaving. Now who's in that house?"

"My father and a soldier and-uh-uh-her brother." Yael was looking at Galit nervously. "Don't go in! The soldier will kill you!"

"One soldier? That's all? I'll take care of him!"

"Wait!" Yael grabbed his cloak, "Don't!"

Then turning to Galit with a pitying look, "I think your brother's dead."

"Gidon dead? He can't be!" Now it was Galit who turned white. Her heart sank. "How?"

"That brute pounced on him when he came in."

"The soldier? Nobody stopped him?" Galit was beside herself.

"Why were the soldiers there?" Eliram demanded.

"To ask questions... and beat us," Yael murmured.

"Beat you? Why?"

"They suspect us."

"Of what?"

"Of what happened in Modi'in."

"Were you there that day?"

"Not until it was over. They've tortured us for hours,"

At that Eliram asserted loudly, "We've got to get to your father and Gidon."

When the children thrust open the door, Gidon was lying on the floor moaning. The two men, Bar Jonah and the soldier, were locked in a hand-to-hand battle with the huge soldier overcoming the smaller man.

The minute they were inside, Eliram flew into action. Aiming his dagger at the soldier's throat, he ordered, "Let that man go! Now!"

The colossal soldier relaxed his hold ever so slightly and began looking around.

"Where's my partner?" he yelled.

"We've taken care of him," Galit answered.

"Let go!" the soldier cried crossly. "Let me out of here and you'll never see me again!"

That was the cry they all wanted to hear but what would he do once he was free? Return with more men?

Bar Jonah tightened his grip on the soldier while Galit and Eliram came alongside, helping to hold him down. Looking at him squarely, Bar Jonah demanded, "What assurance can you give that you'll never return?"

The man was silent while the others held their breath. Then he spoke, "Look, I'm just a hired soldier. I can work for you as well as for them. Pay me my wages and I won't return." Honor and loyalty didn't matter to this man. Money was all he wanted.

This made things easy. Yet, gold and silver were

scarce among the Judeans. Bar Jonah had very little. He looked around his meager dwelling, wondering. What did he have to give? Bar Jonah searched frantically in his mind for something to satisfy this greedy man.

All this time Gidon lay on the floor in a painful heap, moaning from time to time. Now he struggled to sit up. He had an idea.

"Here, take this," Gidon offered the soldier, loosening his watch. "This is very valuable. It's a watch. Nobody has ever seen anything like it in these days. You can sell it and get rich."

The soldier gazed with fascination as the second hand ticked 'round and 'round. When Gidon let him hold it, he kept turning it over and over, then checking again to see if the second hand was still moving.

"Put it to your ear!" Gidon urged.

When the soldier heard the ticking he was more excited. To him it was a wonderful toy.

"I'll keep quiet about all that happened. Just let me have this wat-wat – "

"Watch!" Gidon helped him with the word.

"Waaatshch," the soldier repeated.

"Here! Take it!" said Gidon.

He took the watch and they followed him with their eyes as he arose and went out the door. They were hoping – praying – that he would keep his word.

The soldier gazed with fascination as the
second hand ticked 'round and 'round.

A WELCOME AND AN ESCAPE

It was a late night for everyone. There were wounds to clean. Bar Jonah had received a dreadful gash on his skull, as well as smaller cuts and bruises. Gidon had a bad cut on his right thigh from a clay pot that had been crushed under the weight of the huge soldier.

Under cover of darkness, Bar Jonah and the two boys dragged the dead soldier into the woods so he wouldn't be found. There they covered him completely with leaves, branches and dirt.

When they were back in the house, Yael served everyone dried figs, nuts, dates and grain cakes with a delicious hot stew. The meal was a feast and, for a few minutes, they forgot their troubles.

There was much to talk about. The more Eliram and Gidon told Bar Jonah about Judah Maccabee and the guerrilla training, the more he wanted to join.

"We only have a handful of men. There's no way we can meet an enemy force head-on," said Eliram discussing the Maccabees' strategies, "but we can buzz around them like flies and do a lot of damage to their ranks."

"They've got a huge army, armaments, horses, camels, chariots, even elephants," Bar Jonah responded, "but most of their men are mercenaries from distant lands. Judah's men are local and know the terrain. That gives them an edge."

"I know," Gidon agreed. "The Greeks' soldiers

hardly care if they win or lose. For us it's life or death!"

"It could work. It could work!" Bar Jonah exclaimed.

"And we're going to win!" Gidon said, casting a knowing look sideways at Galit.

"How can you be sure?" Yael looked puzzled.

"They're talking about their histree bucks," Eliram explained, remembering what they said the first night. "But I know something better. The God of Israel will help us!"

"I believe that," Bar Jonah agreed with a light in his eye. "I'll die for the Torah if it comes to that!"

They talked more about strategies and what they could do to win the Temple back. Everyone felt better until there was an unexpected pounding on the door. Just hearing it drained the color from their faces. Bar Jonah went at once to the corner of the room and removed a large stone from the floor. Then he signaled to them to come over. To the children's amazement, there was an opening in the floor big enough for a man to crawl through.

"Move fast, children! Hide down here!" he whispered urgently. The black hole didn't look inviting. The thought of jumping into that pit gave Galit goose bumps, but she and the others did as they were told.

"It's not so bad," whispered Yael, leading the way. "I've been here lots of times."

As the children touched down on the damp, cold ground, they heard the pounding again. Only now it was louder and it echoed off the walls of their underground hideout. The children shuddered with fear. Where they landed they could only crouch, shivering in the dark, huddled among the stones and piles of loose dirt, trying to figure out who was pounding above.

Bar Jonah quickly put the large stone back and threw something over it. It was almost completely dark below except for a sliver of light that seeped through a tiny gap between the stone and the opening. Gidon thought he heard rats gnawing on something, but he couldn't see a thing.

Gradually their eyes grew accustomed to the dark and the one small crack of light helped them see where they were. The place that seemed like a pit at first, proved to be a narrow passageway. They couldn't see where it was leading, but Gidon was sure he saw one of the rats, a grey, clumsy creature, scampering in the shadows.

Sounds were filtering through from the room above. They couldn't tell if the man who'd come in was a soldier or a neighbor. He spoke roughly. He was cursing. They thought they heard the man talk about a soldier found dead. The horror of the words chilled them. Then they heard clearly, "We suspect a roving gang of rebels. We'll catch them! Tell us what you know!"

They couldn't pick up what Bar Jonah said, but could hear something about someone "from Modi'in" and "anyone connected." Then they were sure they heard the words – "will die."

The children's hearts thumped. Gidon was shivering badly. He started to sneeze, and the others pounced on him, all three at once, to muffle its noise.

The two men were talking more quietly now. What they were saying was much harder to hear no matter how they strained to listen.

"What if Bar Jonah gets killed for letting us into

the house?" Eliram whispered under his breath.

The children couldn't catch anything more until the stranger said loudly, "Keep your eyes open, Bar Jonah. Report any prowling strangers." Then, to their relief, they heard the door close behind him.

"He's gone!" whispered Gidon.

"Shhh. He may not be," cautioned Galit.

"I heard him shut the door," whispered Eliram.

"I know who he is," Yael announced.

"Who?" Galit and Gidon both asked at once.

"A neighbor we don't like. He's with the enemy."

"I know him, too," Eliram surprised them by saying.

"You do?"

"How do you know him?" The others were amazed.

"It's Julius's uncle!" Eliram went on. "I'd recognize that voice anywhere."

"I'll kill him for siding with the enemy!" Gidon cried out.

"Better not!" Eliram cautioned. "He's got a lot of power in this town."

"What was that clammy dungeon you put us in, Bar Jonah?" Galit wanted to know, once they had climbed back above ground.

"The 'dungeon' is an escape route. I'm preparing a secret tunnel for days ahead," Bar Jonah answered.

"We're different from a lot of the Judean farmers in this town," Bar Jonah went on. "Some build their homes around pagan altars, like the Greeks. They've forgotten what it is to be Jewish. Your friend's uncle, isn't the only one, Eliram."

Bar Jonah was sorry he couldn't let the children spend the night, but he gave each a sleeping mat of woven reeds to take with them. When the way was clear, the children from Modi'in were smuggled out of the house. They could sleep near the place where they would meet Judah and Eleazer the next day.

Parting from their new friends wasn't easy. Nothing that happened that night had dampened Bar Jonah and Yael's enthusiasm about joining the Maccabees.

"Can't we come along and join your drills?" pleaded Yael.

"We're supposed to report back by ourselves," Eliram hesitated. "Judah and Eleazer Maccabee have to personally choose those who join."

"Yes. That's what Judah said," Galit agreed.

"Come on, you two! We came here to find more loyal Judeans for our drills!" Gidon urged.

"Children, put your worries aside," Bar Jonah settled the matter. "Yael and I can't come until we've brought in the harvest. When that's done we'll load up the donkeys and bring food with us for the people at your camp."

If we still have a camp by then, Galit thought to herself.

PREPARATIONS AND ALARM

In a dream, time does not move fast. It flits away as a cloud on a summer afternoon. This is the way time passed for the three children after that first expedition to Zichron Moshe. Gidon and Eliram were now posted as intelligence spies on Bar Jonah's farm. Part of each crop of grapes and grain brought in from the fields was sent by donkey to the base. At the moment, Gidon and Eliram were trampling grapes in the wine presses and collecting the rich flow of juice into large earthen jars.

Bar Jonah had completed his guerrilla training and Yael had grown three inches taller in height, and miler taller in courage. She and Galit, as relay runners, often carried strategic messages between the villages. Judah and his men periodically attacked enemy units. The guerilla strikes were having their effect.

Eliram and Gidon had been trampling grapes for hours. The bright purple juice was spattered up to their knees, when a runner appeared before them, breathless.

"An army of thousands is coming down from the North. Report to base at once!" The two boys looked at their feet and legs which were drenched in crimson, grape skins squishing between their toes.

"Report like this?" Eliram asked, astonished. He and Gidon looked at each other and laughed. But the boys knew the message was an order, not a joke. Whatever they had been doing, they must stop and set off at once through dry, rocky country to the base. They had to move at top speed. Before starting, they could only take off their damp cloaks and fill their water jugs for the road. For washing and scrubbing there was no time.

Stickiness from the grapes chafed like glue between Gidon's toes, as the boys set off on the upward path. Eliram felt it, too, but gave it no thought. Gidon suddenly felt a pang of longing for one good bath like the many he had refused back home. He promised himself that he would never balk again at taking a bath.

The boys plodded doggedly. Tiredness tugged at their legs, but they couldn't slow down.

"It's rough serving with the Maccabees," Gidon sighed, breathing heavily.

"But I wouldn't trade it for anything, Gidon."

"I wouldn't either, not now when the invaders are afraid of us."

"Right! It's only thanks to our guerrilla attacks that we can now run on this path in broad daylight."

"The enemy patrols we used to dread never take this route any more."

"But it's not getting easier," Eliram called back. "The army pitted against us now is the biggest we've ever faced."

"Still, we've got them worried. If we can beat them this time, they'll really be afraid!"

"I'm not sure we can, Gidon. All the farmers Judah's trained don't come to half their number. Judah wouldn't meet them in open battle."

"Don't be too sure! Remember what I told you. We win all the battles before we get the Temple back. It's in our books. Judah may risk it!"

"It's good *you* know, Gidon. I'm not so sure. But

it's clear God gives Judah his strategies. That's worth more than the histree bucks!"

The boys trudged on and reached the base shortly before sundown. It was not a minute too soon.

PLANNING THE ENCOUNTER

Gidon and Eliram were hoping to find Galit and Yael before the battle began. As it turned out there was no time.

"Here are two intelligence spies from Zichron Moshe," an officer notified Judah, brusquely.

A major action was being planned. Judah was organizing ambush units. Fighters, disguised as farmers, were arriving on foot by twos and threes from the towns and hamlets. Some were chosen for the guerrilla maneuver, others were sent back to their farms and commanded to stay on high alert.

As the boys waited for their orders, they overheard men talking.

"The Samarian commander, Apollonius, is moving this way with over two thousand men."

"But Judah is choosing only a few hundred fighters!"

Hearing them, Gidon and Eliram were perplexed.

"This is sure going to be a different kind of battle!" Gidon exclaimed.

"Strange. Now that we have fighters, Judah should use all the men we can get!"

"Boys! Boys!" Judah suddenly turned to the two. "I want you to come along to the planned battle site. From there you will set out northward under cover of dark. Hide where the enemy sets up camp. Crouch in the underbrush until morning. Make sure not to be seen!

And don't get caught!

"When the enemy starts marching, find out everything you can – the formation of the troops, their numbers, their weapons! Make sure you discover the route they take when they break camp. It should be the road I'm expecting. Then make haste to come back. I'll await your report."

As the sun was setting, Judah called together his small band of fighters and bellowed loudly.

"Be not afraid! Though we be few in number, we have the power of the Most High! A few can overcome a great army. Victory depends not on the size of the battle force but on strength that comes from Heaven!"

As usual his deep booming cry vibrated thunderously and echoed off the distant hills. His fighters then answered with a loud, "Amen!"

It was only at that moment that the two boys spotted Galit and Yael among the band getting on their way.

"Galit and Yael, what are you two doing here?" Gidon asked, amazed.

"We're being posted with the slingers," Yael answered in haste.

"You? You're girls! You can't fight men's battles!" Gidon called running after them frantically.

But Eliram caught his arm, "Gidon, don't stop them! They're needed. They're fine marksmen. If Judah wants them it's because they're good."

So the girls set off with the fighting men.

SETTING OUT

When Eliram and Gidon reached the planned battle site, it was a narrow gorge with steep banks on both sides.

"I see now why Judah didn't choose more fighters," Eliram commented, looking the place over.

"There's not a lot of space here for men to take cover," Gidon agreed.

"It's a long shot to think our men can overcome those mighty troops."

"Judah says it's not the numbers that count but the trust our men have in God!"

"Okay. So let's keep going up this road. We still have to find out where they've laid camp."

It was dark and tension was high, with the huge enemy force so close and coming closer. The boys pushed themselves to keep running for another few hours.

"Look, Gidon! See that smoke curling up into the midnight sky?"

"Looks like we've caught up with them."

"We sure have. Their tents are spreading all the way to the ridge!"

"Let's not get any closer. Right here's good enough to hide in the brush and check their movements in the morning."

The prickly undergrowth was not comfortable bedding, but exhaustion overtook the two in another moment and they lay there, half waking, half dozing, until the morning .

Not many hours later, Gidon and Eliram were startled out of their sleep by the sound of the enemy's marching. Each foot soldier was tight on the heels of the man ahead. Their spears were flashing in the morning sun, mostly pointing upward, but the long, knife-sharp lances of those in the front ranks were directed straight forward. Soldiers on horseback rode alongside the armed men. They too carried lances and swords. The boys guessed that the army was now four hours from base, moving forward in formation at their present pace. Gidon felt a cold sweat chilling his chest.

The boys hastened to return to Judah and the narrow gorge ahead of the marching men. When they arrived, they were both trembling as they delivered their report, but Judah remained calm. He knew what he would do and nothing surprised him.

"You're right, boys. Our fighters are easy prey for the attackers on level ground. But in this gorge we will surprise the Samarian general!

"You two have done well. Return now to Zichron Moshe and remain on high alert!"

RAVINE MANEUVER

The ravine wound back and forth between the craggy hills, only slightly north of Judah's base. His fighters were posted where the ravine began, as well as where it ended. When the enemy marched into the ravine, Judah's men would launch an avalanche of slingshots and pointed stones. At the end of the narrow pass they would attack just before the marching men emerged from the gully. When all the troops had entered the gorge, the signal to attack would be given. The rear guard ambush unit would then rush quickly to seal the entrance to the snakelike pass, blocking their retreat. Judah planned to trap them in the narrow gorge. Their mighty armor and weapons would be useless in such a crowded space. No gleaming swords nor lances would help them.

Judah's fighters had no sooner scaled the steep slopes and crept behind rocky boulders then the marching troops appeared. At first they were like lines of glittering ants, moving across the horizon. Quickly they grew to full size. Line after line poured over the earth's rim, marching in broad formation.

The sun was bright on the craggy heights and Judah's men crouched low, motionless, trying not to breathe aloud. Even a falling stone could send out the alarm as the troops drew near. Horses were already galloping along the road below, turning this way and that to test the lay of the land. Their banners were waving in the noonday breeze. After them came the foot soldiers, marching four abreast.

Galit and Yael were posted as slingers with the ambush unit at the front of the gorge. Their hearts were thumping loudly as the marching men approached. The moment the signal was given, they hailed an avalanche of sharp stones down on the first foot soldiers to appear. The next minute the Judean guerrillas, armed with daggers and farm sickles, began pouncing on those in the front ranks, in hand-to-hand battle. The girls continued raining a hail of sharp stones at the infantry as they came forward. There were shrieks of distress and a shrill whinnying of horses. The animals bucked and pranced wildly.

Down beneath them on the winding road Galit and Yael watched as their Judean fighters attacked and wrestled with the oncoming men.

"They're trapped in the gorge!" Galit whispered.

The soldiers were struggling to maneuver their long lethal swords, but they found no room. Row after row, their troops kept coming. The men moving forward were bewildered as the blockage of bodies grew dense. They could hear the battle cries of their men ahead of them in the narrow pass.

"They keep crowding in," Yael agreed, "and they can't even turn back!"

"Because Judah's men have already sealed off the rear!"

Turning her eyes away from the mass of men being mangled on the path, Yael cried, "I'm getting out of here. I'm sick!"

"I know it's awful to look at," cried Galit, "but

The girls continued raining a hail of
sharp stones at the infantry...

we've got to stick it out, while we're still needed."

"Not me! I'm getting out of here," cried Yael as she struggled to hoist herself upward on the rocky slope.

At that moment Galit caught sight of a magnificent, black horse bounding forward among the enemy's men.

"Look! Yael! It's the general!" Galit cried out.

The next minute she knew she never should have said that.

As Yael looked around she lost her foothold and began sliding backwards. Galit tried to grab her but she was out of her reach. Then Galit lost her balance and had all she could do to keep herself from falling, as she grabbed for roots and clutched at thorny shrubs, their sharp needles digging deep into her palms.

Firmly grasping the thorn bush she was holding onto, Galit steadied herself, ignoring the spurt of blood between her fingers. Then she peered fearfully down on the havoc below to see what had happened to Yael. But Yael was not there. Where was she? Trampled beneath the tangle of battling men? Galit held her breath and cried out desperately. She couldn't go on without Yael. The thought struck her that Yael might be dying this moment and she was icy with fear.

"Yael! Yael!" she shrieked, forgetting the soldiers, the battle and everything.

Then she saw her! Or was it Yael? She wasn't sure. The bright sun reflecting off the rocks and dancing from the flashing swords, confused her. Was it only imagined? It didn't make sense that Yael should be lying over there. She hadn't fallen in that direction. Yet, off to one side, there she was, sprawled in a heap on a narrow ledge just above the fighting men. Blood was seeping through her tunic onto the stones.

What had happened to her friend she could not tell, but at least she could see Yael was moving. As she watched, Yael sat up, slowly steadying herself on the stony ledge.

"I have to try and get to her," she said under her breath. "Nothing else matters."

In the meantime, more was happening in the gorge below. The general had rushed forward to discover what was causing the problems. As he bounded forth on his stately steed, guerrillas on the slope spotted him and let their arrows fly. The general was dealt a deadly blow and his body fell like a stone from his gilded mount.

Horrified whispers passed up and down the ranks among the enemy's men, "Our general is dead!"

"Yes, he's dead."

"Apollonius is dead."

Foot soldiers began running in all directions. It was a bedlam.

They cried, "Get out and run for your lives!"

"The battle is lost! Let's get out of here!"

Some scaled the cliffs. A few stood their ground and kept on fighting, but most tried to flee. Yet, the great army was trapped in the narrow pass. It was like a huge elephant attacked by swarming bees – trapped – trapped – trapped!

SUCCESS AND SORROW

Yael and Galit were dragging their hurting bodies, step by step, back to base. The way was not long but they thought it would take forever. The two hobbled side by side, Galit doing her best to support Yael whose right thigh had taken a terrible beating. Sharp rocks jutting out from the steep slope had gashed it deeply as she fell.

The girls spoke little as they trudged along. They could think of nothing but the sight of the fighters they had seen lying face downward in their own blood or turned on their backs with glazed eyes staring at the sky. On the stretch of road where the battle had raged, Galit recognized one dying man as the father of the lively, beady-eyed Becca, who had given her the slingshot on the trek from Modi'in. Seeing him filled her with a hot rage over what had happened.

"Battles are horrible," she cried out. "Horrible for everyone, whether you win or whether you lose!"

After that the only thing the two girls talked about was how Yael had ended up on the ledge when she fell.

"Yael, you've got to explain again how you landed way over there!" Galit insisted.

"I've told you all I know! I wish you'd been watching."

"I couldn't look at that moment. I was falling, too! Tell me again what happened."

"Someone caught me and carried me over to the ledge where he said I wouldn't fall. I thought it was one of our fighters."

"Rescuing you from the flashing swords and trampling horses in all that havoc?"

"It might have been an angel."

"...unless...maybe it was Becca's father who got killed when he rescued you," Galit shuddered.

"It couldn't have been! My rescuer was the biggest man I ever saw!"

"I don't know. So maybe it was an angel. I wish I'd seen him, Yael."

After that the two were silent, thinking about it.

When Galit and Yael, limping and hurting, finally made it back to base, their hearts were heavy. The triumph of winning a battle was small comfort for what they felt.

Word had gone before them. As they approached they heard sounds of dancing and singing among the women. But not all were joyful. There were women who hurried to meet them with drawn faces, anxious to see if their men would return.

Judah Maccabee came over beside them later that day, saying they'd performed their battle tasks well. But neither of the girls felt like heroes. Yael knew if she hadn't turned coward, she and Galit wouldn't have been hurting and aching as they were now. The marvel of Yael's rescue was the only good thing they could think about in the midst of all the sorrow they felt and all the heartache.

A TIME FOR PLANTING

The sun was shining its morning rays on the Judean hills and the birds chattered busily as the girls made their way out to the fields. Wild iris along the path, like porcelain chalices delicately painted, were sparkling with dew.

Galit and Yael walked gingerly, taking care not to damage the precious bundles they were carrying. The girls had watched, watered, and waited caringly for the seeds to sprout and grow. Now at last they were plants sturdy enough to be set out in the field. Nothing must happen to harm them!

The ground, too, had been made ready. Working until their arms and shoulders ached, they had cleared away stones, coaxed the plodding oxen and prepared the furrows.

"These plants are so small and helpless. How can they ever grow to tough, woody vines, Yael?" Galit asked.

"They will, but it'll take a long time. Some won't make it," Yael answered.

"The way it is with the men in our battles? Some make it. Some don't," Galit mused with a sigh. "I wonder if we'll ever be able to say we've won for good over the invaders,"

"That's a strange thing for you to say, Galit," Yael said. "You're the one who always talks about the histree bucks. Funny that just when I'm beginning to believe what the bucks say, you stop believing."

"The history books? I know, but it's different when you live through it yourself. You and I have seen men die and go down fighting. It isn't the way we learned it in school."

Then the girls were quiet. No one said a word, while they remembered the horrors of what they'd seen.

Galit was first to speak again. "Our men have won another big battle, anyway, since the one we fought in. Nobody dreamed we could win that one, too. Things *are* looking better. But the more they get better the more they get worse."

"I know. And the King sends a stronger army every time."

"That's what I mean. First it was Apollonius. After he was killed, General Seron came down from the North with an army twice as big. Our men beat them at Beit Horon."

"Galit, a lot of it was because Judah and our men prayed. Maybe angels helped, too."

"I don't know about the angels."

"What about the angel that rescued me?"

"I never saw him, remember? I'm glad we've been ordered back home. We won't be fighting next time either. I'd much rather help your father plant the vineyard."

"The Torah says we don't need to join the battle if we're planting a vineyard. That's fine with me."

"But the boys are still in there doing their part! I'm proud of Gidon and Eliram. They do a great job spying and reporting. Look, Yael! Your father's there in the field, already!"

CAPTURED BY MERCHANTS

Gidon and Eliram were just returning from their latest scouting endeavor. Tensions were high at the Judean base, hastily set up at Mizpeh. Rumors buzzed back and forth among Judah's fighting men.

"The Seleucid army has orders to wipe us out!"

"Not one of us will be spared!"

"That's not quite right. They plan to sell some of us as slaves!"

"Not me! No one's going to sell me!"

So the rumors went. What was certain was that a Seleucid army had marched into Judea, twenty times bigger than any they'd seen before. Two generals were in command, one named Gorgias and the other, Nicanor. Gidon and Eliram had been sent to spy out troop movements and report back.

"Judah, General Gorgias' army is coming this way!" Gidon announced, breathless from his running.

"They've left their base at Emmaus with five thousand marching men!" Eliram went on, excitedly.

"And another thousand on horses!"

"From what we make out, they will march through the night!"

"And be upon us by dawn!"

"Sooo... They've learned from our strategies, coming under cover of dark." Judah responded with his usual calm. "They won't be upon us, boys. Don't fear!" he continued. "We will launch our own attack. When they arrive we won't be here."

"Launch our attack? But, Judah, how?"

There was no time for long explanations. Judah wanted his orders carried to the ranks at once!

"Light some small fires, men," Judah commanded before breaking camp. "These will mislead Gorgias into thinking he's caught us unaware!"

Judah paused before setting out, to cry out to God for favor, "that all the heathen may know there is One in Heaven who saves Israel."

Then the Maccabee army set off with Gidon and Eliram among them. "No one stays behind!" Judah had ordered

The terrain was rough for the two boys, exhausted from their heavy running and spying all that day. Nonetheless, they pushed on and kept going as far as the approach to the enemy base.

"Eliram, look at that crevice in the hill!"

"I see it. Looks like a cave."

"If we creep in there we won't be missed."

"So let's do it! We're not armed to join the fight."

So saying, the two boys crept inside the small cave and in a few minutes were sound asleep.

When the battle raged Gidon and Eliram missed the action. Judah had planned a surprise attack on the base at Emmaus. It was good timing. There would be several thousand less men to deal with – the men who now were marching toward his own deserted base. Yet, the size of the enemy force they must meet was still enormous.

Judah had divided his fighters into four units. He put his three brothers, Simon, Yochanan and Jonathan, each in command of a unit, and he himself commanded the fourth. They planned to descend upon the enemy camp from all directions, taking them unawares. However, when they sprung their attack the enemy army was in full battle array and the combat that followed was fierce. Only hand-to-hand fighting determined the outcome. Nonetheless, the Maccabees persisted and the enemy was routed.

While all this went on, Gidon and Eliram were still sleeping peacefully in their cave. Amongst the enemy were local merchants, hoping to buy Israelite captives for slaves. When the battle turned against them they fled for their lives, cursing all the while.

"By Zeus, these generals are bums and cheats!" said one such slave merchant as he ran.

"They're filthy liars to bring us here only to flee!" answered his partner.

Bruggies and Lucius were fuming because of their bungled business. The first, Bruggies, had a small, owlish face, a bulging belly and a deep scar over his right eye. He ran with a lumbering gait like a prize fighter, ready to pounce on whomever blocked his path. The second, Lucius, was tall and slim, with a smooth, dark-skinned face and a wiry mustache. His green eyes twitched nervously when he spoke.

The two men were fleeing headlong, with a string of three donkeys. When they reached a small grove of trees, they stopped long enough for each one to mount a donkey. No sooner did the little donkeys start trotting along, then the two let out their fury against them, digging their heels into their sides and lashing them with their whips.

"Faster! Get on there!" Bruggies yelled, roughly.

Only the third donkey, secured with a rope and trailing behind, escaped the angry lashes of the whips.

No matter how the men beat them, the donkeys refused to speed up. Finally Lucius announced, "It won't help, Bruggies. These donkeys don't have the strength to do better. Let's get into that cave and rest them a bit."

The minute the two merchants reached the mouth of the cave, their greedy eyes fell upon Eliram and Gidon, unsuspecting and sound asleep.

"Ssh! Two Israelite boys! They'll do well enough for slaves!" Bruggies breathed in a whisper.

Without hesitation, the two silently began to work, fastening the boys with fetters, binding their arms and their legs.

They had strapped Gidon firmly and started binding Eliram, when he woke up.

BOUND AND FETTERED

"Hey! What are you doing?" Eliram cried out, frantically fighting to free his arms. Lucius had only begun to bind his legs, when Eliram opened his eyes and saw what was happening. He screamed at once and began kicking at Lucius.

"What's going on?" Gidon cried out, blurry-eyed.

"You two will bring in a tidy sum when we sell you at the market," Lucius responded with a wry smile.

"The market? What market?" Gidon was appalled. He had never heard of a slave market and at that moment he didn't even know if he was dreaming or not.

"We're taking you to the market in Jamnia tomorrow, soon as we can strap you onto our donkeys."

"You'll do nothing of the kind! We're not slaves. We're free men!" Gidon cried indignantly.

"Sorry boys. You're not free now," Lucius insisted with a cynical scowl.

"You'd be surprised. If I could free my legs I could outrun both of you!" Eliram exclaimed.

"But you won't free them, boy! Don't give it a thought," Bruggies answered with a sly grin. "Stay there now, both of you, while we make ready the donkeys!"

"Don't get any ideas, boys! We'll be back before you can blink!" Lucius added, forgetting he hadn't fully secured the fetters on Eliram's legs.

"Quick!", Eliram whispered, "If I can get my legs

loose, I can make a getaway. If I can just pull my knee out of this noose. There! It's coming! Now, I've got the other leg free! Play it cool when they come back. We'll pretend to give up. When I catch them off guard, I'll make a dash for it."

"Come on! Don't leave me! I don't want to be sold as a slave!"

"It's our only hope. I can't even get my hands free. At least if one of us can get running... I can make it to Zichron Moshe by dusk and be back in Jamnia with Bar Jonah and the girls by sunrise. Shhh! They're coming. Just relax and lay low! We'll come get you."

Relaxing and laying low was the last thing Gidon felt like doing.

"Can this really be happening?" Gidon was asking himself. "Being sold as a slave? At the market? If it's a dream, I wish I'd wake up."

But there was no waking up. He tugged at the fetters wound tightly around his arms and legs, but nothing loosened.

"I guess it's good that at least you can get away," he muttered despairingly. "I can't even move."

At that minute Lucius and Bruggies turned up again at the mouth of the cave.

"I'll handle the small one. You grab the bigger boy!" Lucius cried, gripping Gidon by the shoulder and dragging him out of the cave. Bruggies was about to lay hands on Eliram when the boy kicked him hard in the belly, knocking the plump merchant to the ground.

"No, you don't!" Eliram cried loudly and struggled to his feet. With his hands still tied tightly, the boy made a dash out through the mouth of the cave and was off at lightning speed. Bruggies bellowed with anger as he pulled himself back up, but by the time he took up the chase, Eliram was well on his way.

Bruggies pursued, breathing hard and panting, but the fat merchant was no match for a well-trained runner like Eliram. In the end he gave up trying, and returned to Lucius and the donkeys and their one remaining captive, puffing and cursing all the while.

THE SLAVE MARKET

In spite of the early hour, the day was getting hot at the market place in Jamnia. The whole world seemed alive with geese and roosters cackling and squawking, and the bleating of goats and sheep. Gulls, swooping in from the sea, were scavenging for bits of rotting food, and people were milling everywhere, smelly with sweat. Mules and sheep crowded in on each other, trampling in their manure.

What sickened Gidon most were the flies. He envied the mules who could at least swish them away with their tails. Gidon, his wrists stinging and blue from the fetters, could only jerk himself wildly from side to side to prevent them from settling on his nose and in his hair.

He had been doing a lot of thinking during the long, jolting donkey ride with his merciless captors. All the dreams he'd had of becoming a hero had dissolved in a puddle of mud. How low he had sunken! He was about to be sold as a slave! And Gidon heard that most people who bought slaves, were Greek officers or Hellenistic Jews, made rich by preying on their fellow Judeans. His eyes swelled with tears at the humiliation of having to serve such people.

People were gathering now. The slave auction was about to begin, and Gidon had given up hope that his rescuers would show up. He was one in a group of nine men in fetters, some of them young boys like himself. There were those with shiny black skin, brought in by ship from faraway lands, and others of a fair complexion, clothed in patches and tatters. Some looked so pale and sickly, Gidon wondered how they could survive through a day of hard work. It was Gidon's ill fortune to be first in the line.

The marketplace in Jamnia – *Jamnia* – the name kept ringing in his mind. Now he remembered! This was the name in olden days for the modern town of Yavne, near Tel Aviv, where his dear family lived. He longed to be back there and wondered if he would ever see them again.

The pounding of the auctioneer's hammer jolted Gidon back to the moment in all its horror. Bruggies came up from behind him and, first tweaking him on the cheek, he took a firm grip on Gidon from the back of his neck and pushed him forward for the crowd to see.

The auctioneer cried loudly, "This is a healthy, strong boy, worth at least three silver shekels. Who'll bid three? Come right up! Make your offers! He's good for long years of service. Anybody for three? Who'll bid two?"

Gidon was making the ugliest grimace he could, hoping no one would bid at all, when he looked up and noticed Eliram, Yael and Galit enter the crowd. His heart leapt for joy. They had made it after all! But where was Bar Jonah? His eyes searched desperately through the crowd trying to find him. What could those three do without Bar Jonah's help, to rescue him from these heartless men?

"One silver shekel! It's a great buy, friends. The boy's worth his price!" the auctioneer cried again.

At this, a Greek officer stepped forward in full

military dress. "I'll buy the lad for half a silver shekel. That's about his worth," he asserted. With a condescending nod, he stepped forward to close the deal, the silver coin in his hand.

"Going for half a shekel. Half a shekel! Who'll bid more?"

"I will! I'll bid fifty silver shekels and more than that! He's worth a lot more!" a shrill, girl's voice came piercing through the crowd. The next instant Galit was shoving and pushing her way through the throng to get to Gidon. People were gazing at her in amazement. Eliram and Yael were pressing their way through as well, close at her heels.

Eliram's mouth dropped when Galit called out her bid. "Galit, what are you saying? You can't pay that!"

"No, but I've got this," she answered, holding up the CRONOS block that had already begun rocking. She dashed forward and grabbed both of Gidon's fettered hands. Then called out loudly, "There's been a terrible mistake, everybody. This boy's my brother and he's not for sale!"

The next second, the two children were lifted, sailing up into the air, and were carried away in plain view of all the people who looked on, astonished.

...the CRONOS block had
already begun rocking.

A BRIEF RETURN

"Galit, we're home again!"

"Yes, and in Amos' room, of all places! Shhh! Let's not wake him!"

"My fetters are gone!"

"They probably fell apart as we passed through the years."

"Am I glad to be free and to be back here, too. I didn't know if I'd ever see this place again!"

"It feels good, doesn't it?"

"Sure does. But, Galit, we haven't finished the job. Funny the CRONOS block brought us back."

"I know. I think the CRONOS block is like a compass that keeps us on the right track. When we go too far off course it starts rocking. You can't believe how great I felt when it started up at the auction!"

"You felt great? How do you think I felt?"

"Probably even greater. The main thing is you were rescued."

"I know. By the way, thanks for saying I was worth a lot of money. I never heard you say that before!"

"I never thought of it before. You sure see things differently at a time like that."

"I wouldn't want you to be sold for a slave either. I wouldn't wish it on anyone!" exclaimed Gidon. "But, Galit, there's something else that's strange. While we were in the time of the Maccabees, over a year passed. Looks like here it's just been a couple of hours."

"Oh-Oh! Look at Amos!"

In their excitement the children had raised their voices, and now Amos was sitting up in bed.

"What are you two doing here?" he peeped, half-awake.

"Nothing, Amos. Go back to sleep!"

"I wanna' know what you said!" he insisted, wailing.

"Shhh, Amos! Quiet! You'll wake up Mom and Dad! Settle down and we'll tell you!" Galit urged him softly, straightening the covers on his bed.

"Amos, Galit and I have been helping Judah Maccabee fight his battles. We've been back there in those days."

"And we're probably going back again," Galit continued.

"We haven't gotten the Temple back yet."

"I wanna come with you!" Amos insisted.

"Amos, you can't. It's too dangerous," Galit said. "We came back this time because Gidon was being sold as a slave. It was terrible."

"Yes, and once we were thrown up in the air by a big, angry elephant!"

"Whoops! The block is rocking again, Gidon! Take my hand!"

"I wanna come with you!" Amos screamed, reaching to be picked up. But when he looked around, his sister and brother were no longer there. They had been lifted up, right through the walls of the house, and were whirling and twirling and tumbling through time and space.

When they landed on their feet they were in the same spot they had left behind a short while before. But now the market place was deserted – no noisy crowds, no milling animals, no slave auction. Only the flies were still there, buzzing over a pile of manure and there were a few broken fetters laying on the dung heap.

The moment they touched down, they began looking around for some sign of life and, almost immediately, Yael turned up, breathlessly running toward them.

"You're back! You're back! Eliram! I've found them!" she cried. In another minute Eliram, too, came running toward them.

"Gidon and Galit, are we glad to see you! We've been looking everywhere for you!" Eliram cried.

"We weren't leaving Jamnia without you!" Yael insisted.

Then there was hugging all around, but only for a minute.

"We weren't the only ones looking for you! We've got to get out of here!" Eliram warned nervously

"Yeah. Lucius and Bruggies are angrier than wolves."

"They're still prowling around here?" Galit asked, incredulous.

"Come on! Let's get out of here!" Gidon cried in a panic, recalling in a flash the whole misery of the slave market.

"Yeah, before they find us!" Eliram agreed, and with that the four children were off for Zichron Moshe, running at their fastest pace.

A VALIANT VENTURE

In the year following the close call with the slave dealers, Gidon and Eliram were given more important tasks by Judah who believed the two had grown wiser from what they'd been through. He kept them busy relaying messages between the villages or escorting food caravans to the men. Judah's army was growing all the time, and the boys were eager to get back to the heat and flurry of battle.

"I'm glad we've been called to base." Gidon announced as the two moved quickly along the path they now knew well. "General Lysias is launching a new campaign and Judah has a job for us!"

In faraway Antioch, the Greek capital, leaders were angry because of their defeat at Emmaus. Now the King's top general, Lysias, was leading a huge army to Judea all the way from Antioch, to personally "wipe out the rebels".

"Our spies have reported the biggest army yet!" Eliram asserted. "And some of their men are mounted on monsters."

"What monsters?"

"I've heard they're huge, with little tails behind and big ones swinging from their heads."

"Tails on their heads? Strange. They could be trunks and not tails. Are they big and grey?"

"So I've heard."

"Then they could be riding on elephants.

Remember the elephant that almost killed Galit and me?"

"I never saw him, but he must have been terrible."

When they arrived, the two reported to Judah for their orders.

"Boys, we need your shrewdness as spies to learn the enemy's plans. Discover their tactics! You will have to mount horses. Their army is moving down the coastal plain on a roundabout route. We must halt their advance! Our men will move south as you follow their army. Find out the enemy's route. Discover an ambush spot where we can intercept them! They must not reach Jerusalem! I'll send a patrol to pick up your report. Look for him in Hebron, at dawn. Be quick now, boys! Make ready your horses!"

The thrill of carrying out another major task made the boys' blood run warm. They were flushed and excited as they made ready their horses. Yet neither knew how they would manage. Judah's commands would be hard to follow.

"Eliram, do you understand Judah's orders?" Gidon cried out.

"I sure do. I'm just worried about how to carry them out," Eliram answered uneasily.

"We can't talk to the people in Idumea. They're not on our side. So how can we find out where General Lysias is heading?"

"If we could talk to some of his foot soldiers," Eliram suggested.

"That wouldn't help. They wouldn't know anything. Only the officers would know the general's plans."

"But we can't talk to them! They would put a sword through us!"

"If we could find an officer whose morale was low," Gidon suggested.

"How would we do that?" Eliram asked dubiously.

"I don't know." Gidon answered, shrugging his shoulders helplessly. "I'm going to ask the God of Israel to help us," he sighed, stroking the shining mane of his sturdy, black horse.

Both steeds were Arabians, captured in battle – swift and graceful. The boys felt like princes mounted on their backs.

"Gidon, we'd better set off. If we're going to find a way, it won't happen while we sit here!" Eliram shouted jerking his horse's reins sharply and heading down the path.

With this, the boys were on their way. So far they were riding through the Judean hills but they knew they would have to turn westward to find the marching men.

No sooner had they reached the coastal road than they heard the clamor of marching boots. They could also see swords flashing and light reflecting off thousands of helmets, line upon line, as far as their eyes could reach.

"There they are all right!" cried Gidon, his voice quaking.

"Let's follow them from a distance until they pitch camp. We're not in a hurry," Eliram suggested. "When they stop for the night, we can slip down among them in the darkness to find out what we can."

The boys slowed down to a trot, riding along casually, following the road. By now they had been riding for hours. The shadows were growing long as the golden ball of the sun dipped closer to the line between earth and sky.

All at once Gidon grew alarmed. "I don't see them any more up ahead! Eliram, where are they?" he cried out.

"I don't either. Let's catch up with them!" Eliram replied.

The boys dug their heels into the sides of their black steeds and broke into a gallop. Yet, as far as they rode there was no army in sight. They turned and rode in the other direction but still they found no one.

"I can't believe this," cried Gidon pulling his horse up short. "Were we following an army or not?"

"They weren't just ghosts, Gidon. They've got to be somewhere," Eliram answered boldly, though he felt just as confused and uncertain as Gidon.

"We've got to think this through," Eliram decided. "The whole army has changed course."

"But where?"

"I don't know. We've got to find out!"

With that the boys turned impulsively to the left at the first road they came to. From there they just kept riding, slowly and uncertainly.

Both boys were beside themselves.

"What if we don't find them? I don't want to go on," Gidon wailed at one point. "We can't disappoint Judah!"

"Gidon," Eliram suddenly sounded brighter, "Come on! I know this road turns north at Hebron and leads to Jerusalem. It could be the one they took. Say, Gidon, do you see smoke rising along the crest of those hills?"

"Where? Yes. So?"

"They've pitched camp there!"

"You're right! There they are!" Gidon announced excitedly, as they rounded a bend in the road.

"They're camping beneath that ridge. Those are their fires! What did I tell you?" Eliram answered, overjoyed.

As the boys drew near to make sure they had found the army, Eliram spoke up again, "Gidon, do you know what this means?"

"It's great. We've found them."

"It means more than that. We've found them on the route they're taking tomorrow!"

"Just what we needed to know! This is a road to Jerusalem. Now we can give our report to the runner at dawn!"

"Slow down! We only know *part* of what we need to tell him. We still have to find the ambush spot for the attack."

"And that part won't be easy. The terrain here is a lot less hilly than in Judea. No ravines and almost no gullies."

"And also, we have to find out what their men are thinking. We need to get into their camp and spy on them!"

IN ENEMY CAMP

"Quiet, Gidon! You're making too much noise!" Eliram whispered. The crackling of a branch or a stone sliding could give them away.

"I'm hardly breathing," Gidon answered, defensively.

The two were near the thousands of tents stretching far into the surrounding hills. Fires lit after dark, were smoldering to ash. The boys had waited a long time before venturing into the camp. Now the time was right.

"This way!" Gidon motioned, creeping past tents making up the rear guard.

"Let's stop here!" Gidon whispered, as they tiptoed up to one tent. Lowering themselves to the ground, they put their ears to the animal skin covering, straining every muscle to listen.

As they crouched there barely breathing, nothing happened for a while. Gidon was getting shifty, wanting to move on when both boys were startled by a sudden sharp cry from inside the tent. The soldiers woke up and began shouting, one louder than the other. Someone was screaming of wild animals and fiery weapons.

"Listen to them shouting!" Eliram whispered.

"What are they saying?" Gidon asked who didn't understand their words.

"Someone had a dream that they were being attacked."

"So why are they shouting?"

"They say it's an omen from their gods."

"Are they all saying that?"

"Sounds like it. They keep saying it over and over."

"I've heard enough. Let's get out of here, Eliram!" Gidon signaled.

It was none too soon. Awakened by the commotion, men began stirring in other tents. Some had come out to see what was going on. The boys were spotted as they dashed off.

"They're after us, Gidon! Run!" Eliram whispered hoarsely.

Lurching over tree limbs, crouching in shadows, scuttling past barriers on the path, the boys made their getaway. Nor did they let up the chase till they had shaken off the pursuers. Then they trekked stealthily back to the clump of bushes where they had tied their horses.

When they reached the horses, they found them grazing quietly as though nothing had happened. As soon as they saw the boys, they began pawing the ground impatiently. The two boys simply sunk down to the dry ground, exhausted.

"We made it!" Gidon sighed.

"It's good we found out about that soldier's dream. We've really got them scared!"

The boys were so tired now, they only wanted to shut their eyes and sleep through the night. Huddling among stones and prickly shrubs wouldn't have mattered. But they couldn't doze off. Their job wasn't yet finished. They could just lay there a few minutes catching their breath.

Then Gidon, who was getting along now without a watch, looked up at the sky. "I'd say it's just past midnight. That gives us a few hours more before we meet the runner."

"Let's get going," Eliram insisted, shaking off the brush and dirt. "We've got to find that ambush spot! Judah's men need to be in place before the enemy starts marching. Their army is not going to reach Jerusalem!"

"Not now when we've got them worried!" Gidon agreed, shaking off his drowsiness.

The boys hoisted themselves onto the horses and began heading west toward Hebron, searching for the right spot. Yet, as far as they rode no place seemed right. They were both struggling to stay awake when they arrived in Hebron.

"What do we do now? It's almost time to meet the runner," Gidon shuddered.

"Just keep riding, Gidon. We can't meet him without our report," Eliram answered, sad but determined.

"But where do we go?"

"Where the road turns north we follow it."

They kept on riding for what seemed like hours. They were both running out of hope when the path began dipping downward and growing narrow.

"Gidon, do you see where we are? We've ridden into a gully."

"I guess so," Gidon answered yawning. "What of it?"

"Look at the dense shrubbery on both sides! Don't you see it?"

"See what?"

"This is a good place to give cover to our men!"

"You're right! It is a good spot!" At once Gidon was wide awake again.

This was all it took. The two turned their horses around and headed back toward Hebron. Both were excited. The night air was exhilarating and they weren't tired any more. When they arrived in Hebron, a man was there waiting. A man they presumed to be The runner.

"What word do you have to pass on to Judah?" he asked.

"We have heard what the foot soldiers are thinking. They are fearing our attack," Gidon shouted.

"And we've found a gully for the ambush," Eliram continued.

"If you've found an ambush spot, tell it to me! I will bring the word to Judah," the man continued.

Eliram was beginning to feel unsure about this runner. Who was he? There in the darkness they couldn't recognize him. He had the look of a stranger. Neither of them could make out if he was wearing the dark blue cord on his tunic which Judah's men wore.

"How far is it to where Judah's men are camping?"

"A half hour's ride."

"We'll go with you and tell Judah ourselves," Eliram suddenly insisted, motioning to Gidon to follow after. "You lead the way!"

THE HARDEST BATTLE

"Say, what's going on? Where are you taking us?" Eliram yelled at the runner.

The boys looked hard at each other. The more the darkness gave way to day, the clearer it became that this man was not leading them the way they wanted to go.

"You're just taking us in circles!" Gidon shouted to their guide.

This was not the runner Judah had sent. Both boys sensed it. It was a trap. Was this someone who had seen them when they were running from the enemy camp? Maybe one of the men who had chased them? Who could tell what he was up to?

Eliram pulled his horse up short. "You're not taking us any further! Do you hear?" he cried, unsheathing his dagger for a fight. "Watch out! We have orders to kill any traitor who crosses our path!" Then, signaling to Gidon, "Come on! We're heading back to Hebron!"

Their "guide" backed off at the threat of a fight. He simply turned and left. Retracing their path back to Hebron, the boys, to their great joy, found their own runner there waiting. This time they knew the man.

"Peace, brother! We're glad to see you!" they called out almost at once. Judah's runner had been delayed by a number of obstacles along his path, but now he explained how to get back to the camp. Then Eliram hoisted the runner up behind him on his horse, and the three rode off at a gallop.

As soon as Gidon and Eliram delivered their report, Judah's men were ready to depart. Before the first rays of dawn had fully lit up the day, the guerrillas took up their posts on both sides of the gully. This happened only minutes before the steady marching of the enormous enemy army began to be heard from afar.

Eliram and Gidon crouched there, tense with excitement. On cue, their fighters let fly an avalanche of spears and arrows from vantage points above the gully. The oncoming soldiers were caught in the middle under fire from all sides. Men's bodies were falling on the path, blocking the foot soldiers' advance. The boys watched it all unfold, caught in a spell by what they saw. More and more marching men kept coming and were caught in the barrage. It was the general's lead unit and they were taking a beating.

As they crouched there in hiding, the exhaustion of what they'd been through began to catch up with them. Gidon was nodding. Maybe he slept. What he saw when he rubbed his eyes a little later, made him think that he was indeed dreaming.

He nudged Eliram excitedly. "Look! Do you see what's happening?"

Both boys were wide awake now. "I'm watching." Eliram answered, "but I can't believe my eyes. They're all turning around and heading back!"

"Galit! Yael! Good news!" called Gidon banging on the door.

"Better than ever!" added Eliram, panting and out of breath.

Both boys were pounding on the door of the little house in Zichron Moshe but no one answered. It was the same door Gidon had banged on so urgently two years earlier. Then everything looked hopeless. Now both boys were full of excitement.

But Galit and Yael were not in the house. The sun was already low in the western sky but they were still at work. The harvest had been plentiful this year and Bar Jonah needed their help.

Disappointed, the two boys sat down to wait. They had come a long way and the minute they threw themselves on the grass, both felt the weariness in their bodies from all they'd been through the day before.

"They won't believe it when we tell."

"We wouldn't have believed it either."

"The King's star commander gave up easier than we thought."

"And now we're going to take the Temple back!"

"Why don't those girls come?"

"Ouch! My shoulder aches!" Gidon was first to complain.

"If we could get inside, there'd be food there. I'm starved," Eliram went on.

"We could get in through the tunnel."

"We can if no one sees us," Eliram said cautiously, taking a wide look in all directions. "No, Gidon! There's someone in front of that house."

"Which one? Julius' uncle's house?"

"Don't you see him, Gidon? Oh no! I think it may even be Julius!"

"That pudgy fellow outside the door? Is that Julius? The kid who beat you up?"

"It sure looks like him. I feel sick. If it's Julius, I don't want to see him. Why don't the girls come back?"

"If he comes over, just slug him!"

"I could but I don't really want to."

"Then say 'hello' as though nothing ever happened. He's probably forgotten. Maybe he's ashamed now."

"Julius? Ashamed? He'll never be ashamed. He's a bully!"

"But, Eliram, things have changed since that happened. His family buttered up the invaders and got lots of favors. That's the only reason they took their side. Now the King's almost defeated. Don't forget, his uncle changed sides and asked to join Judah's guerrillas."

"Now that Judah's men have started winning, everyone wants to join. But Judah doesn't trust his uncle. And I don't trust Julius. Shhh! He sees us! Oh no! He's coming over!"

"Talk to him, Eliram! What's wrong? You're the bravest of the two of us!"

"Not now, Gidon. This is my hardest battle. I'd rather risk my life spying than confront Julius."

"Well, he seems to be coming this way. Go on, Eliram! Talk to him!"

Eliram bit his lip hard, debating. Finally, he got to his feet and started walking toward Julius. He could feel his heart pounding in his throat as thoughts came back of the blows the boy had dealt him. He felt sick all over at the sight of those plump fists, as he remembered them punching him again and again in the stomach and face.

ENEMIES AND FRIENDS

Julius was first to speak. "What are you doing here, Eliram?"

"I'm just reporting on the battle." Eliram forced himself to speak. "What about you?"

"Helping my uncle. Who's your friend?" Julius asked as Gidon joined them.

"This is Gidon...a fellow fighter with Judah's men. You're helping your uncle, huh?"

"My uncle's got business for the King. I'm giving him a hand."

"Your uncle doesn't know whose side he's on. First he wants to join up with Judah. Then he betrays him. Are you like that, too?"

"No. But I'm not like you. I'm surprised you're not dead by now! I'm not going to die for no reason."

"For no reason? Standing with Israel's God is a good reason! You'd be happier if I were dead, wouldn't you, Julius?"

"No-o-o," Julius replied sheepishly, "but people like you don't live long. You should know that."

"I do know. I don't need to live long, if I die for the right cause," Eliram replied staunchly, gazing scornfully at the grand-looking houses across the way. "A lot of people here give up all their beliefs for the King. How can they live with themselves as Jews? How can you live with yourself?"

At this Julius looked more sheepish than ever. He

didn't answer, he just gazed off in another direction, avoiding Eliram's eyes.

After a while he blurted out, "You and your family bet on the right side, Eliram! We never thought the Judeans stood a chance."

"Bet on the right side? What's that? We didn't bet on any side! If you serve Israel's God, you serve Him. Don't bet on sides!"

"But the Greeks have a lot of things that are better than ours."

"Better? Like what?"

"Their gods and goddesses are something else."

"What's that – 'something else'?"

"Powerful, I mean. Powerful."

"Who says?"

"Don't believe that, Julius!" Gidon broke in excitedly. "Their gods can't do anything. They're not even real."

Ignoring Gidon, Julius went right on, "And their art and their statues."

"What about them? Do you worship statues?"

"I don't. But people do."

"They do? 'No graven images'. That's what the Torah says. You've forgotten!"

"Maybe. But I've changed a lot, Eliram. Judah is a burning light. You can't help changing when his men beat armies five times their size."

"For sure! We just keep hammering at them," Gidon exclaimed.

"Judah keeps 'hammering', just like his name, Maccabee, the hammer," Julius agreed.

"Right! But Julius, that's not it either. You've

missed the point," Eliram insisted.

"What is the point, then?"

"It's that any of Judah's men would die in a moment. That's what serving the God of Israel is about. We serve Him and He fights our battles."

"That part I don't understand. Sorry, Eliram. You and I still don't see things the same way."

The three boys had been sitting on the grass, talking for almost an hour when Galit and Yael showed up. They were still far off, two small figures drawing near across the fields. Talking with Julius hadn't been so bad, after all. Eliram thought he *had* changed. He wasn't as mean and arrogant as before. Gidon also thought Julius wasn't as nasty as he'd expected.

Now Yael and Galit were practically in front of the house.

"Eliram, stop talking! They're here!" cried Gidon. "Yael! Galit!" he called, waving frantically. "We've got great things to tell!"

Eliram made no move to get up. He was sitting quietly looking at Julius, just gazing at him. A great weight lifted from his heart. He and Julius had been talking in a friendly way and that in itself was a great thing. There was still plenty they didn't agree on. But he couldn't remember ever being able to talk with Julius on friendly terms, at least when each one listened to what the other had to say.

"If you want, Julius, you can stay while we tell the girls about Judah's latest triumph," Eliram said casually. "Stick around!"

ON TO THE TEMPLE!

It was the day they had all hoped for, though few dared to expect. Judah's men were getting ready for their greatest expedition, to take back the Temple. A band of guerrillas at the base were preparing to leave, and the children were already on their way. The yellow clay road they walked on was no more than a pathway, cracked and dry. It was a road beaten down by the steady plodding of countless feet over many generations. The air was chilly but it didn't matter to the children. They were singing and their hearts were cheerful.

"We're lucky Judah chose us for this important job," Gidon said and whistled as he kicked at a mound of gravel on the path.

"It's great for Yael and me, too," Galit chimed in. "This is the first time Judah has sent us ahead for advance scouting. If there's shooting from the walls of the fortress, we'll be there with slings and arrows."

"What about you, Julius? I never thought Judah would want *you* along," Yael said bluntly, turning to the pudgy boy.

"Me? Why not?" Julius answered, indignantly. "I know some rich Jews in Jerusalem who could help us. We may need some help while spying things out."

"Does Judah really believe you've changed your mind about our cause?" Yael was puzzled.

"He knows I've changed my mind about a lot of things."

"A lot of things? Like what?"

"Like God's Laws."

Eliram was also worried about Julius.

"Make sure you don't give us away to your rich friends, Julius! They'd all betray us."

"Working with the King! Betraying our people! That's what your friends do! I wouldn't go near them! They shouldn't be called Jews at all!" Gidon cried out angrily.

"I've told you I've changed! I'll tell them, too, if I have to!" Julius was looking fierce now. He was really different from the thoughtless bully he had been.

"You believe in Judah's campaigns now, don't you, Julius?" Yael asked looking surprised.

"Why shouldn't I when Judah wins every time against bigger armies?"

"God helps us, Julius. But we have to honor His Torah. Don't forget that!" Eliram insisted.

"I can't wait to get to the Temple!" Julius cried out suddenly.

"You have changed, Julius!" Yael repeated, staring at him in disbelief.

"We don't know what the Temple is like now. They've probably ruined it," Eliram pondered.

The children kept walking. They had more to talk about.

"Tell us again how Judah won that last battle," Galit pressed the boys to explain.

"We've told you. The ambush spot we found was in a narrow gully. That's where we attacked and wiped a lot of them out," Gidon boasted, forgetting he had been all blurry-eyed and sleepy at the time.

"Did the whole army really turn around and march back with General Lysius at their head?" Galit marveled.

"All the way to Antioch in Greece!" Eliram exclaimed.

"We watched them turn back at the ambush spot Eliram and I found," Gidon boasted again.

The girls just stopped in their tracks, both gaping at the thought of that huge army doing an about face, elephants and all, for their long journey back.

"That was marvelous!"

"It sure was!"

The girls agreed before moving on.

A minute later Galit stopped to drain the last drops from her water jug.

"We've got to find water. Does anyone else need more?"

"I want to eat from our lunch packs," whined Gidon. "I'm hungry and tired."

"You're always hungry and tired, Gidon," his sister teased. Yet, secretly she felt that this time her brother had really been a hero.

THE FORK IN THE ROAD

"Say, Eliram! Are we going the right way? What are those marks on that rock?" Gidon asked.

Since their lunch break, the children had made good progress. Now they came to a halt at a fork in the road. To Gidon and Galit the markings on the rock were unreadable. For the others they were no problem.

"This one says 'TO JERUSALEM'," Eliram answered.

"What does it say on the other rock?"

"Same thing. They're different routes. That one to the left goes through Emmaus."

"Emmaus?" Gidon cried out. "I never want to go back to Emmaus!"

"Neither do I – Let's not go that way," Galit hurriedly agreed with her brother. "What do you think, Eliram?"

"Well, I'm pretty sure the route through Emmaus is quicker."

"Have you forgotten the slave dealers, Eliram?" Gidon answered, dumbfounded.

"Sure I remember," said Eliram. "But the important thing now is to get to Jerusalem as soon as possible."

"You can go that way if you like," said Gidon stubbornly. "But you're not going to drag me along!"

With that, he set off determinedly down the other path, leaving the others staring after him.

"So which route are we taking?" Julius asked

impatiently.

"I think Gidon has decided for us", Eliram shrugged. "We'd better catch up with him. But we still have a long way to go."

The children ran to join Gidon, but they didn't get much farther that night. Before long, everyone was yawning and too tired to walk fast. Dusk was covering the area with its blanket, so the children laid out their sleeping mats under a small grove of trees and prepared to spend the night. One more day's journey would bring them to the gates of the holy city, and they were all eager to get there.

ARROWS, VIPERS AND THISTLES

It was late the next day when the sturdy, majestic walls of the Jerusalem came into view. The children had no trouble entering through the gates. There were no soldiers anywhere. But when they came to the Citadel, the enemy fortress, they had to duck and run for cover. Speeding arrows came from every direction, flying down from the walls and whirring up from the ground, raining between the garrison above and Judah's guerrillas below.

It didn't take the children long to piece together what had happened. Judah and his men had arrived ahead of them and were already battling the enemy at the fortress. Though the Seleucid soldiers were closed up in their Citadel, they had plenty of weapons. Judah would not try to recapture the holy city now or penetrate the fortress. For this he would need a much stronger army. He just wanted to make his way past the stronghold and arrive at the Temple.

The children knew that Judah intended for some of his men to hold the enemy at bay, so that the rest could go forward.

"Didn't I say we should have taken the other road?" Yael pouted.

"You said that but not until the next morning when we'd gone a long way on that road," Galit reminded her.

The others agreed she should have told them sooner.

Gidon knew he'd been wrong to insist on that road but he didn't say a word. He still hated the thought of going back to Emmaus. Eliram had known it was the wrong route, but Gidon hadn't listened.

But Julius was glad they'd come the longer way. Since they'd arrived late they wouldn't have to fight. The guerrillas were doing the job already.

None of them wanted to be a part of the battle now anyway. Their minds were all on the Temple. They just wanted to scramble past the towering fortress and make their way there as fast as possible, to explore its ruins and discover everything they could. Galit said there had to be one little jar of pure, sacred oil hidden somewhere in the Temple. If they could find it she was sure something wonderful would happen. Even before getting to the Temple they all had their hearts set on finding that jar of oil.

Only a few of Judah's men were engaged in the battle. Yet, it seemed to the children that none of the others had moved on past the stronghold.

"If we can slip by unnoticed we can still make it there ahead of the others!" Gidon suggested.

Galit was unsure. "Shouldn't we let Judah know we're here?"

"Maybe so. Maybe not. I'd sure like to see the Temple before the others get there," Julius urged.

"Come on now! Weren't we told to go ahead of the others? Those were our orders," Yael insisted.

"But we didn't do the job we were sent for. We were supposed to spy out the enemy ahead of the others," Eliram pointed out, sensibly.

"I'm going anyhow," Yael announced abruptly.

Then, without asking more questions, she broke into a run and off she went.

The other four stood there speechless.

"She can't go alone like that! It's dangerous!" cried Julius.

"I'll run and catch up with her," Gidon cried out. The next minute he was on his way, too.

Galit was beside herself. "What do we do now? What will happen to my brother? And what about Yael? She can't always expect angels to help her!"

At this Eliram took the lead, deciding for them all. "Listen, you two, there's no time to stand here talking! If we don't go after them now anything can happen!

It didn't take the four children long to catch up with Yael. They reached her at the entrance to the outer courtyard, or where it once had been. The gates to the courtyard were ruined and burned. Three of the children had been there before but they weren't even sure they had found the right place. They had all come up to the Temple with their families for the holy feasts. But now everything was changed. The magnificent structure was reduced to rubble and the courtyard was overgrown with brambles and thistles.

The five children were pushing their way, single file through the brambly undergrowth, Yael still in the lead.

"It's completely deserted!" wailed Yael. "There's nothing here at all."

"Except these thorn bushes," Julius added, looking around for recognizable signs.

"It sure doesn't look like our most holy place," Galit sighed despondently.

"Yikes! There's a snake!" Yael shrieked suddenly.

"It's a viper, Yael! Don't move! It's coming toward you," Gidon cried under his breath.

"Watch out! There's another over there! The place is full of them!" Eliram signaled in alarm. "It's a viper, all right, Yael. Nobody move. He's ready to strike. Galit, get your slingshot!"

"I have it!" she answered trembling.

"Now aim! Take only one shot! Don't miss it!" Eliram cautioned.

She let it fly and the shot struck. The children couldn't see quite where the sharp stone hit its mark but the stunned snake uncoiled and slithered away, leaving a sticky, reddish trail behind it.

"Good work!" said Julius admiringly, as he and the others breathed again.

The children were still shaky, Yael most of all.

"I don't want to go on!" she wailed.

"You don't?" Gidon asked perturbed. "You're the one who wanted to set off ahead of Judah. Maybe you want to go back to the Citadel?"

Yael didn't answer. She only stared down at the brambles and patted her scratched and bleeding legs.

It would have made sense for the five children to return at that point and report back to Judah. But that was the last thing any of them wanted to do, except for Yael, who had lost her nerve.

"Who wants to go back? We've gotten this far. We might as well go on!" Gidon announced boldly.

"This place isn't at all what we expected," Galit objected. "It looks more like a haunt for owls and dragons."

"I can't understand what my father's friends have been doing," Julius considered mournfully. "The priest the King put in charge gets paid to take care of things!"

"Your father should be more careful about picking his friends. The King probably pays that priest to let things go, Julius," Eliram answered sharply.

"Why did we ever come ahead of Judah and the others?" Yael wailed.

"You were the one who wanted to, Yael," Galit reminded her.

"We all ran after you, Yael," Eliram pointed out, glancing over at Gidon who had also been part of the problem.

"But what do we tell Judah when he gets here?" Yael wailed again.

"Hush!" whispered Gidon. "We're not alone. Somebody's coming."

There were, indeed, men coming – a whole troop of them. They were carrying knives and farm sickles, chopping and slicing their way through the brambly undergrowth.

It didn't take the children long to see the men were their own guerrillas. Bar Jonah was among them. Yael spotted her father. At once she ran blindly through the thorny shrubs, throwing her arms around his neck and sobbing hysterically.

FIGHTING UNDER ORDERS

Once in the Temple, everyone felt downcast about the way it looked. Walls were crumbling and fallen pillars lay in pieces. Altar stones were scattered and the silver and gold ornaments blackened with fire. Almost everything beautiful and holy had been broken. Worst of all were the idols – Greek statues standing in different places with a tall figure of Zeus, like a cruel stony giant, towering above them all. Only the *Menorah*, the beautiful, seven-armed candelabrum, was still in one piece, lying on its side in a corner, covered with ashes and dust.

"They've broken everything!" Galit cried out in horror.

"The smell here makes me sick," Yael whimpered, pressing her fingers over her nose.

They were all feeling about the same. The bottom had dropped out of their fun. Their eagerness had disappeared. Besides, the children were feeling guilty and miserable now for not having reported to Judah when they arrived.

"It won't be easy to explain," Galit pondered.

"We have to tell him everything!" Eliram insisted in a burst of righteous logic. No one else said a word. They all knew he was right. Judah was sure to ask questions. It wouldn't do to pretend they hadn't done wrong.

"We all have to take the blame," Julius announced unexpectedly. This brought on a number of frowns and raised eyebrows. Should Julius be telling them who was to blame? He of all people! A whole argument might have broken out if the children hadn't suddenly noticed Judah was already in the Temple.

He had been surveying the damage with some of the men in an area cloaked with darkness. Now he'd caught sight of the children, and was striding toward them through the debris. Judah hadn't forgotten about the children. He was glaring at them with a heavy scowl.

"Why did you children not perform your tasks?" he asked roughly. Judas' words made them all feel about two feet high. They wished they were somewhere else.

After an uncomfortable moment of silence, Julius spoke up first. "We took the wrong road. We're all to blame." The other four said nothing. Galit and Eliram felt like blaming Gidon. Yael was thinking maybe she should have said something sooner.

"Wrong road or right road, you didn't report at the gate!" Judah roared.

Then Gidon spoke up impulsively. "We were going to but it was already late. We wanted to be first to the Temple."

At this Judah roared at them in a fury. "You were going to report but you didn't! You wanted to be first! You wanted excitement! An adventure, perhaps? Is that how a battle is fought? Are you fighters under orders or not?"

"We are fighters, Judah, under orders," Eliram spoke out firmly, stepping ahead of the others to face up.

But Judah wasn't ready to hear anyone. He still had words for Gidon.

"You, Gidon! You were doing well as a scout.

What happened? What about the mighty warrior you're named for? Gidon – Gideon. He followed orders from God. His men did what they were told. What do you have to say for yourself!" he stormed again. "What do any of you have to say?" he confronted them all.

By now no one had anything to say. There was nothing to be said. They didn't feel like telling Judah they had grown tired of battles and only wanted to go back to being ordinary children.

The color had drained from their faces. Yael was shaking all over, her knees were still puffy and aching from the giant briars and thorns. She was feeling this day had started badly and it would also end badly.

"It's really my fault," Yael whimpered. "I ran off and Gidon came to get me. The others came after him. That's why we didn't report back."

By now tears were rolling down her cheeks. She couldn't hold them back. And Judah was looking into each of their faces to see who was telling the truth.

Finally his angry look grew milder. He, too, was thinking, after all, they were only children. Children who had distinguished themselves with brave actions – yet still only children. After that, each one told his part of the story while Judah listened.

"In battle everyone obeys," he declared. "Nobody breaks rank. By not fulfilling your tasks our strategy was harmed. Men could have died and the battle to regain the Temple could have been lost."

By the time he had finished nobody was dry-eyed. All were shaken and ashamed. Yet, they felt better. They had told Judah everything – or, rather, almost everything...

ONE JAR OF OIL

"You sure put your foot in it!" Eliram declared, nagging Gidon after it was all over. "You didn't have to tell Judah about our wanting to get here first!"

"You're the one who said to tell Judah everything! And anyway, at least I didn't blurt out about the jar of oil," Gidon quipped defensively.

"The whole altar must go!" Judah had commanded. "Where pigs have been slain to false gods, holy offerings may not be placed!"

The children had all gone to work. Many hands were needed to clean up the filth and repair the beautiful ornaments of the Temple. None of them had forgotten the little jar Galit said would be hidden there somewhere. But, Judah was giving them no time to search. Nobody dared breathe a word about it, after all that had happened. Yet, wherever they stepped they were always looking, checking every shattered vessel, anything that could hold oil. Once Eliram unearthed a little pottery jug with his sandal, while exploring a mound of earth. But when he picked it up it was cracked and whatever was inside had leaked out.

The girls were helping repair the colorful woven veil that hung before the Holy place. The stitches were tiny and delicate.

"Getting all these stitches right takes forever," Yael complained.

"It's hard," Galit agreed. "But it will look lovely

when it's done."

"I'd still rather be hunting for the jar of oil," Yael went on. "I guess we've got to stick to this. I don't want to see Judah get angry again."

So the girls worked on, struggling with the stitches for hours.

Julius had been given a very special job. One of the men repairing the gold and silver ornaments was teaching him how to do it. Julius was excited and thankful for the chance to work with these beautiful things. He didn't know quite where the feeling had come from, but deep down inside he wanted badly to make up for having turned his back on the God of Israel. He really wanted to make something beautiful for Him now. There were rings of gold to be hammered out and the lovely flowers on the candlesticks had to be repaired. There were golden snuffers for the lamps and little dishes of gold upon which the snuffers were placed. All needed to be fixed. Some had to be made from scratch.

When the men working on the Altar had finished taking it apart, stone by stone, they built a new one with fresh building blocks that had never been chiseled or hammered. Each stone had to be fitted carefully into the others until the Altar was ready.

While the work on the Altar was still going on, Judah finally let Galit and Yael take a break from their stitching. It was then Galit drew on all her courage and asked Judah to let them search for the jar of oil.

"It's got to be here, Judah! I'm sure!" she insisted. "People in our time sing songs about the miracle of the oil that was found in that jar!"

"Sounds good to me, my young friend, if only it

were true," Judah was cheerful but stern. "I don't think you'll find any such jar. We've sorted through everything. Still, you're free to look for it. I'll give the boys a break so they can search with you."

Galit was beside herself with joy. She leapt in the air, clapping her hands, hardly able to wait until they all could get started.

The boys too, were eager to begin looking. The children hunted and dug in every spot that seemed likely. Their hands got filthy and smelly from the dirt but they found nothing. Galit was sure it had to be there but in the end even she began to doubt. Yael, whose trust in the God of Israel had come bounding back after they'd spoken to Judah that day, believed that He would help them find it. In the end she was the only one who still kept looking, but she, too, at last gave up and decided they would never find it.

There was nothing they could do but go back and tell Judah it wasn't there. He had probably been right. It was just a made-up story that Gidon and Galit had heard about in their days and that people in their time had believed. They knew now the story wasn't true.

As the five children trudged back to the place in the outer court where Judah was working, their hearts were heavy and their heads downcast. When they were only a few paces from Judah, Yael stumbled on something that sent her flying headlong to the ground, scratching her hands and face. She was up again in a moment, but she couldn't understand what she had tripped on and went back to have a look.

The next moment Yael was screaming, as though this time she'd really been bitten by a snake. But that wasn't the reason why she screamed at all.

"Look, Gidon! Galit! Julius! Eliram! Look! Look what made me fall!"

The next moment they were all examining what she had in her hand. It was unmistakable – a little jar all caked with dirt. And it was heavy. As they shook the jar and held it to their ears, each could hear the swishing of liquid inside.

Julius, turning to Yael, said, "Good for you, Yael! I think you've found it. May I see the jar for a moment?"

Yael handed him the jar. Julius used the edge of his cloak to wipe off the dirt and heavy film that had collected. Then he began turning it over and over. Wiping some more, he stared at strange markings on the jar.

Finally he said, excitedly, "There! I see it!"

"See what?" the others asked.

"The priest's own imprint. It's a jar with the high priest's seal!"

"You mean that little mark there? That's the seal?" Yael asked dubiously.

"That mark shows this oil is purified for the Temple?" Eliram questioned.

"I think so," Julius nodded. "If the seal is genuine, this oil can be used to kindle the golden Menorah. It's probably enough to keep it burning for about one full day."

It was unmistakable –
a little jar all caked with dirt.

STILL BURNING

When the Temple at last was cleansed and everything repaired, a great celebration was held. The festival took place three years to the day after the King had looted and spoiled the Temple with pagan offerings. It lasted eight days, with music, dancing and prayers of thanksgiving. There were beautifully-dressed women with golden braiding in their hair, and young men dancing with all their might to the tingling rhythms of the tambourines and the gentle strumming of the harp. The children joined in with all the merriment and rejoicing. Yet, most of the time none of them could take their eyes off the golden Menorah. Its flickering lights burned day and night.

"The flames have already been burning seven days now," Galit exclaimed.

"It's wonderful. We thought the little jar held enough oil for just one day!" Yael chimed in with delight.

The children were standing, gazing full of wonder at the great candelabrum. The flames seemed to be alive and refusing to die. Seeing them brought many things to mind.

"Do you remember, Gidon, when the prophet, Moses, saw fire burning in a bush, and it didn't burn the bush up?" Eliram asked.

"Sure I do."

"It was strange. The bush didn't burn up from that fire."

"I know. That's because it was God's fire and God spoke to Moses from the bush."

"You know what? I think it's something like that with these flames."

"You mean, since the oil doesn't get used up?"

"I think it's God that keeps these flames burning, not just the oil," Eliram murmured.

"I see what you're saying!" Yael commented. "Maybe God's angels are here, too, though we can't see them. Don't forget about the angel who rescued me!"

"I don't know if that was an angel," Eliram responded, "but Judah Maccabee and all of us have this same fire that's in the Menorah burning in our hearts."

"You're right about that, Eliram!" Julius agreed. "It wasn't that way for me before. Since I joined up with you the fire's in my heart, too!"

"You can't put it out because it's God's fire!" Gidon asserted triumphantly. "No matter how bad things get, the fire's still there!"

"Oops! The CRONOS block in my pocket! It's rocking, Gidon!"

"CRONOS block? What's that?" Eliram asked.

"It's the magic block that brought us into your world. If it's rocking that means it's time to take us back. Watch out, Eliram. We may fly out of here any moment!"

"That's not good" Eliram objected. "I don't want you to go."

"Nooo! Stay!" Yael cried out.

"Please, you two!" Julius begged.

"Gidon and I don't want to leave but we probably have to. Here, Gidon, grab my hand!"

"No! I'm not coming!"

"Okay, I'm grabbing you!"

Just as she did this, the two children started whirling once again and twirling up into the air. They barely had time to wave good-bye to their friends before they were both out of sight. Galit closed her eyes tightly as the two traveled through time and space, trying hard to remember all they'd been through and particularly the golden Menorah with its beautiful light.

Gidon finally succeeded in breaking her grip on his arm just as the two landed down. Their landing was not with a thump as at other times. They just felt a soft, muffled bouncing as each one landed inside his own warm, bed, cozy and comfortable, as though they'd never been away. Galit was still gazing in her mind at the small flames, flickering and bright.

"They're still burning," Galit murmured rubbing the sleep out of her eyes and looking around. There was her favorite wicker chair, her own desk and all the stuffed animals. Mother was there, too!

"What's burning, dear? You smell the toast!"

"Nooo! It's not the toast! It's the Menorah in the Temple! The oil from the little jar keeps burning and burning."

"Galit! Stop the nonsense! What are you talking about?"

"It's true. Ask Gidon if you don't believe me!"

Gidon, overhearing their talk, came wandering into the room, stretching and yawning.

"She's right, Mom. We were there in the Temple in the days of the Maccabees. The oil from the little jar we found just kept burning and burning.

"Is that so? You were there? Well, that's a new one."

"Yes, we were. And Gidon, Mother! He really was a hero! You would have been proud of him."

"Really? It's strange when I think of it. Little Amos was screaming about you two last night when he came into my room and crawled into my bed. He kept screaming about you two fighting with the Maccabees. It took forever to quieten him down. Anyway, it's late. You two have to get off to school! Gidon, where's your watch?"

"My watch? I don't know. I can't find it."

"Don't bother looking for your watch, Gidon. You've forgotten, you gave it to the enemy soldier we bribed to keep quiet!"

"You see, Mom. It did happen! We *were* really there!"

"Yes, otherwise you never take off your watch at night, Gidon!" Galit reminded him.

"But, Mom, there's something I want to ask you," Galit went on.

"Yes?"

"What is this?" she asked, pulling her hand out from under the covers where she was still holding the CRONOS block.

"That block? What are you doing with that antique piece?"

"We took it out of the cupboard last night thinking it was a dreidle."

"Well, it's not, so let's put it back where it belongs. May I see it a minute?"

"Yes, but Mother, where did it come from?" Galit pressed, handing it to her mother.

"It's quite a story how I got this funny little piece.

The antique dealer who sold it said there was a mysterious power hidden inside, and that it would bring the right people special benefits at the right time."

Turning it over in her hand, she added thoughtfully, "I guess it was just a sales pitch. He charged a lot for it, but I bought it anyway. It's rather quaint, isn't it?"

"It's quaint, all right, but that's not all. There *is* a mysterious power hidden in this block, Mother! We were just about to put it back in its place in the cupboard when the power hidden inside carried us back to the time of the Maccabees. You have to understand, Mother, what that antique dealer told you wasn't just a sales pitch," Galit insisted.

"It sure wasn't!" Gidon agreed with conviction, recalling the trips through the air, through time and space and through years and centuries. "It was a whole lot more."